J. Henry

The Christian Pulpit: its place and power

J. Henry

The Christian Pulpit: its place and power

ISBN/EAN: 9783741189050

Manufactured in Europe, USA, Canada, Australia, Japa

Cover: Foto ©Andreas Hilbeck / pixelio.de

Manufactured and distributed by brebook publishing software
(www.brebook.com)

J. Henry

The Christian Pulpit: its place and power

THE CHRISTIAN PULPIT:

ITS PLACE AND POWER.

By J. HENRY, A.M.

——————

" .   . *How shall they hear without a preacher.*"—Rom. x. 14.

——————

BELFAST:
1892.

SOLD BY THE BOOKSELLERS.

BELFAST:

PRINTED BY JOHN A. MURPHY, HOWARD STREET.

THE CHRISTIAN PULPIT.

CHAPTER I.

IF the pulpit be of importance in society; if it be, as it professes, a means of instruction; if its grand mission be to
exalt human souls to a higher standard by presenting to their
attention remarkable objects, or conveying to them convictions
which might possess a moralizing effect, then it is essential
that its real object be defined by just and observable limits,
and its efficiency, as far as possible, secured and augmented to
meet the requirements of society in all its ranks and characters.
If this highest result be not secured; if it occupy but a limited
space; if it disdain scientific theories, refined argument of high
and ingenious intellects against that faith on the reality of
which it exists; if it hold in supercilious contempt every conception, save what is in close affinity with theological dogmata;
if it only recognize, as the standard of its exercises, sermons
and volumes and modes of thought produced centuries ago, and
which may, in their day, have been instructive and useful, it
will not be remarkable should its place, as a reformer of men,
manners and systems, be taken by a generation "bringing forth
their fruits in their season." This generation may be regarded
and stigmatized by it as presumptuous and profane, as carnal
and worldly, "as overladen with iniquity," and dwelling in
darkness; but if society was induced to labour under the impression that a chimerical effect only emanated from the pulpit,

and a real one was secured by other instruments, an opinion might begin to prevail among the enemies of the Faith that it was "waxing old," and was part and parcel of a system "about to vanish away."

All the while we know and are assured that among the systematized means of imparting information and advancing the cause of humanity, the pulpit, if it does not occupy the chief, might, by a little painstaking and labour, be made to occupy the highest place. Whether we look to the grandeur of its lessons, the object of all its exhortations, the honoured position it holds in the affections of vast multitudes whose souls are in a great measure exposed to its influence, or the lofty source whence its finest exhibitions are supposed to flow, it will, by the vast majority of people, be demanded that whatsoever "letteth" or impedes its highest usefulness should at once be taken out of the way.

By the pulpit are meant its occupants who, from Sabbath to Sabbath, deliver their preparations to the multitudes who come to listen to them. And here it may be observed that, compared with the press, this great moral power labours under many causes which interfere with, and sadly diminish, we are afraid, its efficiency. When a human being listens to a discourse there are certain drawbacks in the case which do not exist in his perusal of an article from the press. In the former case he is listening to that which the exigencies of his spiritual nature ought to render peculiarly interesting. But he may not be quite sensible of these exigencies. He may not be quite convinced that the exposition about wickedness and sin and forgetfulness of his Maker is for him. He may not be willing to think that he is in such need of a regenerating Spirit and an atoning Oblation as his presence in the sanctuary would warrant us to conclude. It is, perhaps, not so easy to gain access to the seat of his spirit's ruminations as the speaker may imagine. The interests adverted to may, to him, be rather utopian. The soul, encased in the scale-armour impenetrability of mere ephemeral interests, may hardly admit the point of that arrow intended to penetrate that coat of mail. The assault of the man of God upon it, though with all the vigour and *elan* of one who knows his office and wields its solemn power, may be against such a tough and stubborn shield of stupor, misconception and estrangement as may cast a mockery on the attempts of a giant in the ministry of the Word.

But even if a hearer has a sincere and earnest wish to be edified, a discourse delivered with ordinary rapidity is altogether different from a dissertation from the press, which may be, according to taste or feeling, detained before the attention. He cannot, unused as he is to the effort of abstract thought, confine in the crucible of intellect any new or definite argument or exposition until it has, by time, produced the intended effect on his understanding. He cannot command "the sun to stand still in Gibeon, and the moon in the valley of Ajelon." A mass of printed composition may have attention bestowed on its several sentences, according to their meaning and importance. One sentence does not hurry forward on the conclusion of another unless by the reader's own will. He may be imbued by the spirit and substance of each before making his transition to the next. His spirit may exert its critical power as he reads. It may augment or curtail. It may wish the writer were more concise here, more expanded there. It may lament obscurity in one place, or deplore unwise attempts at elaboration in another. Now, little of this can be done with a sermon, and by a large portion of the audience nothing at all. Besides, the very staple and make-up of a discourse from the pulpit is an element that does not enter general thought or calculation. The urgencies of life, its sorrows and business, forbid this. What is intended is, that all these interests put the soul in a posture in which it is not easy for it to listen to such topics, however pressed on its attention. Perhaps, in most cases, other topics carry an overwhelming ascendency. Though they did exhibit the proportion which the six days of the week, given for the performance of worldly business, have to the day decidedly set apart for the purpose of bringing moral natures into unison with the high themes and exercises of immortality, yet when it is remembered that the one set of considerations, besides being so congenial, so palpably pressing, so indispensably urgent, is kept before the attention six continuous days, and is attended

with more than sixfold effect, and that the other set of subjects
come round at intercepted intervals, it will then be admitted
that to bring them before the mind with effect involves no
ordinary talent, preparation and power.

It is true it might be maintained that, in this holy warfare,
the battle is not man's, but God's, and that it is to a Power
irresistible, and who "will perform all His pleasure," that man
has to look. Yet they who have most reliance on this argument
never forget to mention the animated manner, the earnest and
impetuous diction, the burning eloquence, the appeals and arguments of one who truly feels he is struggling with a mighty
power of waywardness; that he is actually in conflict with "the
old man"; that he is labouring to bring to birth and manifestation "the new man"; that he is a champion against "spiritual
wickedness." There is something here which might be called
human. The voice at least is human. The illustrations are
collected by observation. The train of ideas has been previously
arranged. The best words have been carefully selected. The
sermons that have had confessedly the mightiest effect on
society were sermons previously incorporated with the thoughts
of the preacher, without depressing or extinguishing his earnestness. If the Spirit work in this matter, He must be said to work
with advantages which are sometimes natural, such as strength
of voice, copiousness of illustration, propriety of language.

Indeed, the real impellent of the minister must be the Spirit.
The general impulse must have this holy Monitor for its origin-
ator. But it were, we apprehend, a misuse of language to
maintain that the Spirit was not only the motive power, but
that it was the Spirit studied—it was the Spirit prepared the
sermon—it was the Spirit examined the Original—it was the
Spirit dwelt in busy contemplation on the text, until its truths
arose out of their obscurity and expanded themselves beneath
the severe scrutiny of the faculties of the scholar. If any should
be inclined to adopt this view of the matter, it might be time to
say here that we are addressing the intelligent in society, whose
penetration is such that they can recognize "the things which
differ," and not those who so view the Spirit's operations that they
substantially do away with the Spirit Himself, and reduce all to the

actings of the human intellect. If these operations are not the exercise of the intellect, but of the Spirit, they then must be the most perfect of their kind, without blemish or imperfection. But human fervour has its decays and diversities in different Christians, and in the same Christian at divers times. Human eloquence does not always kindle into the same fire. Human souls are not always harassed with the same agitations. The doctrine of the Holy Spirit leaves the power and result of means uninterfered with— leaves each one responsible for stirring up his every faculty by the strongest motives and arguments—leaves to everyone the peculiar features of his own distinctive intelligence; and, instead of acting as a sedative to the human faculties, puts all into motion, and declares that a contempt or disuse of means and effort are excuses only of ignorance or inaction; and that the surest index of His own Divine co-operations is when they work power-fully in leading to the best plans and most effectual ways of doing the work which He assigns them.

Man thus labours, to all intents and purposes, as if he laboured from his own unassisted abilities, and without this Divine Instigator. At the same time, the Spirit is the grand impellent and directive Agent in man's labours. The Spirit gives heart—endows with the noble resolve of employing his powers for the good of the world. This may be His province; and though it were His only province, who would not acknow-ledge that it was enough that, leaving the endowments with which God engifted His creatures in their ordinary state, He gave man taste and inclination to bend and direct his talents to the Divine glory. The Spirit has His functions which He can perform. These may consist in implanting in the mind of man the generous resolve of doing good. Man has his province, which is to employ his intellect and his powers for the glory of his Maker and good of his fellows. Is it necessary to insist on the interchangeable character of these two functions? Does the invisible Agent imbue the mind of the inelegant with a new taste? Does He implant or create new conceptions in the minds of those whose conceptions are naturally destitute of vividness? To those devoid of a bias in favour of some study or investigation in some section of the sciences does He impart ardour? We

are not confounding any taste, learning or aversion with the
conversion of the soul. Do we not find that in the case of those
converted by the Spirit that their faculties are greatly limited,
if they were so before—their minds remain destitute of that
quality by which man is pleased with exhibitions of the sublime
or impressive in nature and art, if they were so before?

The benefit of this admission is, that it leaves us the power
of saying that a Christian may be actually the subject of the
genuine and sanctifying operation of the Spirit, and yet no new
taste or faculty be imparted. His memory may not be invigor-
ated, nor his imagination exalted, nor his faculty of invention
enlarged. This is the case, because conversion does not imply
any such change. There is no more reason for insisting that
such a change takes place in conversion than that it is the
province of the Spirit to change the subject of His influences into
a poet or engineer. If this were the result of His unseen
operations, the rustic would be a scholar, and the ignorant man
a linguist, or the man ungifted with fancy or invention a poet.
In conversion no such transformation has been ever desiderated—
has been ever exhibited. To demand more than professed con-
verts have claimed would be casting a suspicion on conversion
itself.

If, therefore, the Spirit convey no new faculty, but only
make the best of the natural gifts of the recipient of His Divine
influences, it is not to be supposed that what He refuses to the
humble disciple He will condescend to perform for his instructor
and his guide; and, while leaving the power of prayer as the
power that moves the arm of God—while leaving all spiritual
agencies where we found them—it is not to be thought that
without days and nights of labour and assiduity—that, without
a purpose to adorn his calling, and a stern resolve to capture
the prey from the mighty, and make those the bondsmen of
Christ, who were before the bondsmen of Satan, the minister of
the Gospel will ever do so. In general, the power of man on
this field has gone with his fervour and his scholarly attainments and his well-sustained circumspection and his untiring
industry. It is true, he may have been converted. The Spirit
may have even induced a character of such fervour to devote

himself to the task of building up the Christian temple, and filling up the number of the chosen people. But all the while, the Spirit may have not so much imparted the ardour as directed it; may not so much have communicated the vividness of conception as set before it the affecting alternative of souls, either careering to unending ruin or laying fast hold on eternal life.

Where a lively imagination is natural, immortal and unchanging destinies, separated by the dreary and impassable gulf, will be affecting to most men; and, moved by the calamity which appears in the perspective, if they do not repent and enter into peace with God, the activity of the preacher and the pungency of his sacred preparations will be proportioned to the liveliness of his own conceptions. Were he to witness the spectacle of a vast and surging multitude, blindly crowding in the direction of a yawning precipice, over which, he knows, if they fall they are torn and shattered on the craggy projections beneath, it is not unreasonable to suppose that the outcry of this spectator, and his vehemence, should borrow its urgency from the vastness and irreparable character of the disaster. This, we say, would be the natural effect of that transparency of fancy we have referred to. It might certainly be the doing of the Spirit to put him in the position, or to post him on the spot, whence he might survey the procession speeding on to misery and perdition. And we cannot conceive of one witnessing the sight without girding up all his energies for the work of arresting these victims of a sad delusion in their infatuation, or at least making the endeavour to persuade some of them to abandon a path that will surely terminate in their unhappiness and their despair.

The way, we think, has been thus cleared for the statement of the general proposition that, leaving the Spirit's work and His office in their indispensable efficacy, it were a matter of utterly mistaken zeal to affirm that His work is of a nature which obliterates distinctions of talent or degrees of diligence; that here intellectual power is out of place or useless. This were an insult wantonly cast on endowments God Himself has imparted. It were to dishonour the creation of His hands. It were to assert that powers which win so many trophies on other fields are unnecessary on this one. It were to allege that all that is required here is the audacity of headlong and impetuous fanaticism. It were to repel from this sublime work the intellectually and, we venture to say, the morally great. It were to uphold that the contractedness of narrow and bound-up faculties is only necessary here. It were strange, indeed, if the Spirit behoved to be exalted at the disparagement of endowments which God has imparted, or wrought up with the original formation of some of His creatures.

We are not inclined thus to place such confidence on some propositions as their advocates would naturally expect. When people talk of the Spirit's work it is in a manner rather unsettled and indefinite. They do not seem to be conscious that they are speaking of a power awful and mysterious in the extreme. And, while one would be led to suppose from their assumption that nothing was easier than to mark His progress and point to His footsteps, there is more probability that their readiness at concluding only offends the good, and deters the wise, and leads the reflecting Christian to observe that they exhibit little of that "charity" or love which is, at all events, one of the fruits of the Spirit.

In the same way, it would be hardly proper to affirm that muscular vehemence was the only characteristic of a work of grace on the heart. It would seem like to planting a limit around the illimitable. To confine a Divine work to show or to noise were in a manner excluding it from silence and retirement. To say that the soul which is convinced it has found mercy must break out into declamation on the greatness of the miracle would be to depreciate the aids to increased piety, which may be bestowed by time and by meditation. To cast all natures into the same torment and transport would be equivalent to ignoring those natural distinctions discovered in creatures so variously endowed. We conclude, then, that the gracious work of this Holy Visitant is not confined to any grade of intellect or to any particular demonstration; that it will present different appearances, according as it touches on different natures; that, instead of natures being overborne in their tendencies, constitutions being totally reversed, or new intellects created, it consists rather, not so much in the change of the internal, as in the exhibition of a new creation replete with new and interesting phenomena, and which really lies without us. It is not so much the internal which undergoes the alteration. It is greatly the same. New objects have been presented before the internal vision. If there be a change on the internal, it flows from the external. The two domains greatly remain the same. Only the one domain is brought into close proximity with the other. The seeing eye looks outward on objects which were always there, but which it never saw before, because it never considered them before. The eye of the spirit was before shut on that ample and interesting territory. Its eye is now opened, and, as a consequence, it beholds "wondrous things." New regions are disclosed, because the organs are turned in a new direction. It is greatly an exertion of thought expatiating over a region on which it never dwelt before ; and, if there be anything which belongs to the Spirit here, it is inducing the sinner to give attention to those things which concern his eternal well-being, and which, when the eye is opened on them, He invests in colours of impressive and overpowering loveliness.

Nor would we in these remarks wish to cast an imputation on the reality of conversion as such, though we could not concur in many ideas which are current on this great subject. But, strange to say, those who could not tolerate the idea of a church without many and visible instances of this turning of the soul to God, are found sometimes so to restrain it as to make one believe that verily very few are born again. On the other hand, they sometimes make the matter so easy that the venting of a desire, the show of some transient warmth, the ejaculation of a prayer would, so to speak, serve as a sufficient qualification for an immortality of praises. The matter could not be made more obscure than it already is by many who insist on it as a scriptural doctrine, or as an 'indispensable prerequisite for endless development and praises. The reason, perhaps, is that those who speak of these great concerns are not the persons who have themselves experienced the Spirit's work—are those who have never seriously investigated its nature, but are satisfied with the opinions which are popular and current on the subject, and which present the

appearance of orthodoxy or of conformity to some general standard. That their asseverations be agreeable to some formulary
is quite sufficient, even though they have never evinced great
anxiety whether they be reconcileable with reason, scripture, or
general principles of truth. They would rather be thought
orthodox than reasonable. The very term reasonable is
ominously excluded from their theology. And a verse of scripture, which carries on its surface the appearance of vindicating
their peculiar tenets, is quite satisfactory, even though, if viewed
in the light of criticism, it militated against them. How often
are study and research regarded as superfluous! How often are
they so apprehensive of innovation that the labour of study is
avoided, lest haply some new discovery might be fallen in with!
It is not the rigour of examination, but tradition, which has
modelled their opinions ; and their creed is not so much a spiritual
experience or a mental production as it is the submission of
the soul to the modes of thought and speech to which common
custom and language have set the example.

The tenets of theology have thus lost a part of that novelty
by which it is that a new doctrine actually possesses a power of
fascination which by no means belongs to an old one. Without
being directly brought into the moral state which the doctrine
intends, the mind becomes at last habituated to it. Without
examination it accepts the doctrine. Without inspection of its
evidences it gives to it the fullest credit. This, it is evident,
leads to a state of intellect not very consistent with the idea of
responsibility. At first, possessed of that novelty which
delights the understanding, because it presents the mind with
a new class of ideas, the doctrine may have been attended with
an awakening energy, of which the course of years or centuries
had deprived it. In the case of Christianity, we apprehend that
other circumstances have contributed to lower the honesty of its
acceptance without depreciating its value—its value, we mean,
as it stands recorded in those books to which we apply the
epithet "revealed" But if we could state any number that
would represent the value of Christianity, that number would be
the same now that it was in the age of Polycarp or Ignatius. In
connection with novelty there was, no doubt, in susceptible

minds, a something in standing on the very borders of the time in which the first grand Herald of these Divine truths appeared on earth, or in juxtaposition to the localities honoured with His presence. The chamber in which He came as a guest to a marriage; the hill from which He addressed the multitude; the sea on which He stilled the clamours of the tempest; the rocky elevation on which He suffered; or the eminence from which He ascended, no doubt contributed to impart vividness to the objects of their faith. It is not to be supposed that, in view of these favoured localities, faith could be anything else but animated—ready to suffer and to dare anything for a Being so self-denying and so constant.

Leaving out of view those sturdy intellects that repudiate every doctrine that they cannot understand, and scowl upon every-thing like mystery—that regard concealment with suspicion—there is another class who seem to be engifted with a large amount of toleration, and take for granted submission and gentleness. If there be any such fact as general truth, the one spirit may be as much dishonouring to Christianity as the other. The one is impetuous in its dislike of what it cannot understand. The other gives its acceptance most readily to the popular system—to the reigning opinion. The one is revolted by pretensions which demand to be accepted, because they come from a lofty and inaccessible authority. The other at once gives its ready, we can hardly call it its enlightened, adherence to opinions because they have now become a portion of a life-system, and interfere not, at least not in fact, with worldly interest or secular advantage. The one class do not know how they are called upon to submit their inquisitive understandings to doctrines which come with claims so eminent and peremptory. The other class, with minds either not inclined or not at leisure for the disentanglement of histories or inspection of evidences, are rejoiced that they are permitted entrance and initiation into the temple of the Supreme on terms so lenient, on qualifications so complaisant.

We know not, indeed, whether it is perfectly consistent with truths so elevated to condescend to a belief so facile, since all truth, prior at least to its obviousness or discovery, requires

research and time. And anterior to the exercise of the human
mind busied in the task of inspecting histories and evolving
credentials and observing remarks of palpable sincerity, we
know not if any system of truth could altogether be warranted
in demanding unquestioning belief. This remark may be applied
to the grandest system we know of. And that system seems to
make it one condition of its genuine acceptance, that it be subjected to investigation and scrutiny—"Search these books, these
facts, these tidings; search the scriptures if these things be so."
Indeed, it might be said that a body of truth which presented
such claims as that enquiry was dishonouring to the high
Authority from which it came, and it must at once receive the
highest belief of the soul, would itself be exposed to the dishonour of suspicion. An honest commodity, which is what it
represents itself, is positively not the worse, but the better, for
the scrutiny to which it is subjected. The honest intellect will
no more accept any doctrine on mere hearsay than it will give
itself to the turpitude of passing or circulating anything on
mere rumour.

In closing these preliminary remarks, it might be stated that
a prompt acquiescence in the truth of a system merely declared
that it was incorporated with the ordinary forms of custom and
daily business. Now, this might be true with a system which
was secular, and somewhat homogeneous with the customs and
arrangements of "the life that now is." But this criterion can
by no means be applied to the Christian Ethics. Were it some
system of ceremonial etiquette—some ready reckoner in the calculations of merchandize—general acceptance would be a sufficient
excuse for lack of individual examination. Were it the object to
produce the finest polish of manners and utmost propriety of be-
haviour in the parties and entertainments of society, or to abridge
the calculations of the negotiator, all the ardour of sincerity
and the necessity for anxious examination would be misplaced.
But Christianity is something *ab extra*. It has not, at least in
its grandest elements, in its noblest features, been given with a
view to be embodied into worldly systems. In so far as it inculcates honesty, the claims of truth or watchfulness of principle
in all our transactions with the world, its precepts are to be our

guide. But all this is not Christianity. We may hear of this on the page of Cicero. This is certainly indispensable to the Christian character; for the man habitually dishonest in his dealings, and unmindful of truth in his sayings, could not be a Christian.

It must follow, therefore, that the ideas of Christianity, properly so called, have to do with the spiritual state, deformity or waywardness of human souls. It postulates—it takes for granted an abruption of the soul from the original source of its felicity. It is just as if some planet which drew abundance and light from a central sun had, by a collision, experienced such a shock as was sufficient to give it a new orbit; and that, separated from the fountain of its light and heat, its population languished under a climate adverse to their health, which shed a blight over its whole surface, and promised to leave their world a vast and untenanted desert. A system might be granted them that would summon into activity certain qualities, which should enable them to pass their existence in considerable felicity, with the promise that, at the hour of dissolution, they would, on certain conditions, be once more transported into the radiance of their olden orbit, to live for ever in the beams of solar effulgence. This is Christianity. And it surely is worthy of an effort to try and indicate how the utmost efficiency may be imparted to the endeavours of those whose solemn office it is to teach this great system, to unfold and illustrate its Divine truths, to persuade hearers honestly to accept of them, and to travail in birth with souls, until, by their patience and labours, "Christ, the hope of glory," be formed in them.

CHAPTER II.

THE PREACHER'S OBJECT—MAN ADDRESSED AS CAPABLE OF
UNDERSTANDING AND ACCESSIBLE TO CONVICTION.

OUR observations, at present, shall be confined to the
discussion of the object for which the ministry of the
Word has been established, and has actually been commissioned
by a Divine Master in the words, "Go out into the world
and teach the nations." Resting on that Divine commission,
and, in compliance with it, founding all their refutation
of infidel objections and infidel flippancies upon it, a goodly
band of pious men have, in obedience to their great Head,
traversed all lands and erected everywhere the standard of the
cross. This commission of their acknowledged Lord has been
enough to unbind the ties and connections of kindred; to dis-
solve the attractions of domestic life; to counteract the schemes
of profit and selfishness; and to break asunder those many
tender endearments which bind us to the land of our nativity.
These general orders have bidden the missionary ship to unfurl
her swelling canvas to the breeze of heaven and direct her path
to the distant shore on which idolatry has built its temples and
offers its cruel immolations. Apostles, confessors, and martyrs
have, in submission to these Divine words, itinerated over
districts which, before them, never heard of a redemption, and
know nothing of its preciousness or its necessity.

The objection might here be adverted to, that if the Gospel
be a system without which man, as man, cannot be permitted to
approach his Maker—nay, cannot know who He really is—why is
this *gradatim* process adopted; and, like certain tiny seeds
which carry with them certain hairy additions which waft them
softly over the landscape, why, in the same manner, has this
Divine intelligence, whose pretensions are so exacting, and
which has in view the spiritual conquest of a globe, and
which in some way constitutes the happiness of the world, not
been supplied with a mode of conveyance which would place its

advance beyond the capriciousness or the persecution of luke-
warm friends or bitter enemies? We must remember that
according to an arrangement by which any knowledge is
circulated it also is circulated. The message which has been
sent from above regarding man's deliverance is one which can
be best conveyed in the volume in which holy men, employed by
the Spirit of God, left it for our instruction. This has been the
usual way by which these gracious tidings have been successfully
carried from one nation and people to another. Without this
we know not of any method which could plant this Divine seed
in other lands.

Its rise and increase are connected most closely with the
advancement of the sciences and literary refinement. Keeping out
of view the consideration which implies the progress of language
and its copiousness, when the Divine record can be translated
into a new language, it will not obtain possession of a very
wide field without the contemporaneous advancement of the arts
and sciences. The advancement of letters is equivalent to the
advancement of everything lettered and contained in the field of
scholarship.

The achievement dear to the hearts of Luther, Carey,
Williams, and Judson, was to give to the people in that tongue
which was the vehicle of their daily thoughts and tenderest
emotions the Word of the living God. A nation must have
grown into a certain love of refinement and capability of
appreciating grand ideas, expressed not in speech, but in written
characters which the mind might decipher and understand.
The soul of man may be fitted in the lowest state of rudeness
for receiving "the record which God giveth of His Son"; but
this record must be made known to him by words or in writing.
Until a language has been formed in which to make the business
of salvation known it is impossible to find admittance to his
mind for these concerns. The message may be admittedly
interesting; but, it may be said, "how shall they hear without
a preacher"? The intelligence may be all the difference between
an eternity of pain and gloom and one of supernal and everlasting beatitude. But, let it be as momentous as it may, these are
the fitting and preparatory channels by which it must reach the

B

unenlightened or most cultivated soul; and that is either by the vehicle of a living voice or a written word.

Thus, like every reformation, like every improvement, the mode of propagation for that book which contains the mind of Christ is the same. It must necessarily be gradual. And how much it is fitted to give rise to serious and sometimes bewildering reflection when we consider that what God might, by some wholesale process of dissemination, have left as a sacred depository in all the islands and continents of our globe ; what He might have bequeathed as an invaluable gift, not to one land, but to the globe itself; what He might have delivered, unrestrained by limits of time or place, and creating no prejudice on account of nations that first or that last received it, He has been pleased to give piecemeal to our world, and confine, perhaps for centuries, to one despised nation and one petty district. This ought to produce all the glow of an irrepressible desire for its speedy emancipation from the narrow and undignified limits in which it is held, and fill man with all the ardour becoming an enterprise so vast as the subjugation of all lands by the cross of Christ.

But, whether in lands of barbarian superstition or regions of refinement and civilization, the object which the ministry of the Word has in view is lodging the Divine Word in the seat of the emotions—the heart. This is in reference to the ministers of the Gospel "making good proof of their ministry." He that can accomplish the most lodgments of this kind is the workman who needeth least to be ashamed, and most successfully "divides the word of truth."

But so many are the disguises, and such the insidiousness of error; such an incrustation of inveteracy, habit, and lethargy, or satisfaction with some artificial form; such an antipathy to the themes of salvation; such aversion of the thoughts from them to the themes of earthliness; such complacency if the most superficial glance be given at them; or if a single verse of that book which proposes them to the mind be impressed on the memory, that, while the minister's task is considered an enviable and easy one, we might pronounce of it that it is one which demands the energies of a Samson in the cause and all the earnestness of a Demosthenes for its successful carrying to the heart. Those who can think of it as requiring the abilities of a child or its energies are altogether mistaken regarding its weight and meaning. Accordingly, all those terms which denote strenuousness in action, or undauntedness in conflict, or swiftness in the race, are used by an apostle in connection with his apostleship; and, no doubt, the function which he found most difficult in its exercise, and somewhat undetermined in its results, was declaring "the word of this salvation sent" for the elevation and good of man.

It pleased the beneficent Maker to implant in man many and beautiful emotions, and a power of receiving or creating, or intermingling forms and conceptions which he never was conscious of before. We are mistaken if it be not in virtue of these affectionate movements within him, and those shapes and ideas which his intellect forms and apprehends, that he is a being fitted to be dealt with in any moral scheme—capable of receiving an impression from that in which he discerns the marks of benevolence, and of being agitated even to ecstacy at the boundless prospect of a future immortality. These be the powers and the latencies within on which the ambassador of the court of heaven must found the success of his grand mission. Take them away, and you take away the avenue of access to that only part where he is capable of being impelled or arrested, retarded or accelerated, in his pursuit of the objects of faith or of this world.

It is obvious from these remarks that the power of the preacher is just the power of gaining access to these privacies of the inner nature where are stored up hopes or fears, loves or aversions, multiplied waywardnesses, or rapidly rising hesitations, or boding ruminations. To this interior region, which man prides himself in holding in strict guard and reserve—to this recondite concealment, where, in some way, lie those mysterious elements which can be moved into all the throes of an agony which shakes his whole tabernacle—to this place, where repose the germs of future activity or future thought, and which are awakened by the corresponding sentiment carried into the ear by the human voice, to this the minister must endeavour to find his way if he would obtain, for the overtures of eternal life, that hearing of interest with which they should be listened to. This may be considered too abstract a statement of the matter. It is, however, the true one. We do not maintain that it is indispensable to the minister of the Word thus to climb his metaphysical way into the penetralia of man's moral or spiritual nature. But one would have more confidence in trusting his malady to that physician who had penetrated farthest into the secrets of nature, the general root of disease, the principle of life in the human fabric, or the influences of Nature which affect existence.

We know that many, destitute of such knowledge and unaided by such refinements, have, by a happy skill aiding a resistless ardour, held all knowledge that was not absolutely essential in disregard, if not viewed it with contempt. It is seen and acknowledged what these untaught and humble men have accomplished without the learning of the scholar or tastes of the philosopher. We honour them; we give them the tribute due to such merits and endeavours. But it is to be remembered that we do not know what they, if possessed of the aids of learning and models of eloquence, might have done. Knowledge may have abated the ardour of their onward career; but it also may not. Nor do we think it possible to estimate the high position which knowledge ought to occupy in the herald of the cross.

The definite object which such a view of man as the above presents is to point to the exact place to carry which all efforts should be directed. Here lies the crude material which is to be wrought into so many forces—so many impellents or resistants. The knowledge of the exact spot of the disease would be of no small importance in the art of healing. The knowledge of the exact point of weakness in a citadel would be of unspeakable moment to the general whose harassed and sorely exhausted levies have laboured with mine, and countermine, and parallel, and circumvallation against its frowning and rugged precipices. The patient is racked with the agonies of some hidden malady. The doctors muster around his couch in gloomy silence or in busy and low-whispered consultation. All the time the seat of the complaint may have evaded their penetration till one, more used to the observation of diseases and their symptoms, comes in and finds that all their labours were directed to a part possessing the haleness and vigour of health.

To a work confessedly so momentous, what pains will be thought disproportionate? It were tinging the whole business with the air and complexion of servility if the thought were entertained that the labour to be done demanded nothing more than the mere knowledge of what was contained in that volume which is the depository of the hopes and consolations of the Christian. A real taste for that celestial record is seldom found to exist apart from a taste for the productions of general intellect. Nor is this wonderful, since it is intellect which makes its researches, its discoveries, and comparisons, both on the field of earthly and heavenly knowledge. Many are the trophies to the glory of God and incentives to genuine piety on the former as well as the latter field. We are afraid that a distaste for general might, without much argument, be construed into a dislike for all knowledge. To avow such an aversion for what is at least innocent is hardly consistent with the character of him who regards the mind which discovers as coming from the Supreme grand cause—as being an emanation of the Mind Divine. Such an avowal might lead to a suspicion of any very serious, intelligent, or continuous study being bestowed on the Bible. It touches on so many points within the range of general science; its allusions are so many in the field of classic learning; its evidences are so derivable from many and widely separated sources, that a really sincere man will not repute himself worthy of the Christian name if he do not search into them, or worthy of the praise of anything like intellect if he fail to appreciate them.

The ground on which the minister's appeals can be regarded as reasonable, or can be attended with success, is the intelligence and moral accountability of those to whom they are addressed. They are directly addressed to man as a rational being, the unholy elements of whose nature may be subdued by them, and its virtuous aspirations developed and strengthened. Each human being is furnished with a moral nature, though in some it appears to lie in entire dormancy, and long will the

Christian orator wait till he meets with the intelligent look or the kindling glance. Argument and persuasion may, in their turn, be employed without breaking the slumbers of that lethargy which has cast its spell upon their souls. Their natures are fast locked in a sleep or in the vacancy of unideal bewilderment, through the bound-up callousness of which no argument is found to penetrate. Shut up thus in themselves—unconscious of aught save the annoying and petty concerns of daily life, or perspiring the sweat of that ignoble toil which, though laudable and blessed in itself, is sometimes found to quench the bright beam of intellect—some there are on whose nature the weight of argument and urgency of appeal have but little effect. It declares the hardening power of carelessness as well as of sin, and is, perhaps, fitted to give to the minister of Divine life the lesson that he is to summon up every energy within him to the task of making a breach in this indurated strength of habit by assaults well sustained and wisely directed. If any subject requires the effort of solitary thought and long-continued contemplation it is this; and surely it should be regarded as a suitable reward of his prayers, carefulness, and preparation, when he sees, spreading itself over the countenance, the sympathetic look of dawning intelligence, and, where all had been dreary, vacant, and unmoved, to behold the signs of awakening interest and feeling. But still the effort must be plied and persisted in until the object he is in pursuit of be attained. Let him not faint under the weight or apparent inefficacy of such labours, nor be greatly distressed if the wished-for symptoms be not presented as soon as he expected. He must take into account the mantle of "thick darkness" which he is labouring to dispel or draw aside. He must reckon on the strength of habit, counteracted, perhaps, by no opposing habit. After calculating the power of such a defence as this, let him know that, even though his efforts exhibited all the despised form of enthusiasm, there is abundant excuse and abundant reason for them all.

In dealing with the spirit of man, it ought to be remembered that it is possessed of two great implanted faculties—intellect and soul. Both have to become the object of the preacher's attention. The neglect of the one might lead to the mere assent to certain systems, a cold and profitless and intellectual scanning of truth, and a satisfaction with the rigorous formulas of system. The intellect here may be supposed to delight itself with its fertility of resources—its ability to balance truth with truth, and deduce conclusions which may please by their exactness or dazzle by their magnificence. The truths which the sacred orator enunciates cannot be deprived of the power of engaging the intellect. The book which contains them would differ far from ordinary literature if it was maintained that the intellect of man found here no field for the development of its powers or for evolvement of sacred doctrines. It must be submitted to the intellect. It is calculated to exercise the powers of memory, for its verses may be laid up in this repository. The imagination may expatiate amid the scenes of eastern lands passing in review before it—whether it be a steward sent to find a wife for his master's son, or the hoary parent wailing the loss of his favourite boy, or the distressed and beautiful damsel among the gleaners of a harvest field. The judgment may, from the general ideas formed about the probabilities of the Divine economy, or from the discovered qualities of the Divine nature, exhibit its sagacity in drawing up in order the various articles of belief which might be proposed to the credibility of mortals.

Truth, perhaps, is never invested with greater power than when, arising amid the radiant conceptions of intellect, it blends itself with those emotions which play such a part in every-day doing and history. It is here that truth may be placed, with all its probabilities and attractiveness, before the mind. Copiousness of illustration, elegance of language, and employment of metaphors are doing most effectual work when they are used in imparting a new idea for the confidence and direction of a human being. Where it dwells most vividly and substantially in one mind, from that mind it will certainly carry its full impression, rather than from a soul where it has never been rendered luminous, patent, and mighty in itself. It will be able to find so many ways of displaying itself, and so many paths of transmission, that he who sees it most vividly will convey it most effectually. Clearness of vision in the speaker will be indispensable to exactness of representation when he exhibits truth.

But to comprehend the whole man, to take in all the elements of his nature which may be regarded as worthy of the attention of the sacred orator, we must allude to the emotions. These are love, fear, hate, hope, ambition, envy, selfishness, and so many other properties, which to move, to impel, eradicate or control, is the highest aim of the pulpit.

Indeed, conversion itself is appreciably unintelligible if we do not regard it as enlightenment conveyed or emotion produced. If it is some effect with which the intellect or the emotional part has nothing to do, it would be difficult to assign its proper place in the Christian system. It seems impossible that the Spirit of God can shed His influences on creatures fitted to receive them unless by either conveying enlightenment or moving the affections. If He operate on man, it can only be on man as no undefined being or in an imperceptible and peculiar manner, but as compounded of intellect and affection. To convert is, therefore, to give enlightenment to the mind or to move the affections.

What, it may be asked, does this intellectual light consist in when a man becomes the subject of Divine grace, and when God has set His love on him for his salvation? Is it some light really flashed, as a ray, into the region of his mental faculties? We know that to place one in the condition of a beholder we must not only impart to him light: there must be objects on which this light is cast. In the darkness of midnight the whole landscape is wrapped in the mantle of total obscurity. Not an object is visible. What though the landscape be distinguished by flood and field, waving foliage, valleys laden with plenty, and hamlets or mansions embosomed in trees, yet if light be not reflected on its beauties—if they be not made to emerge into visibility by a light shining on them, the power of vision is unequal to the task of beholding them, and the mind dead to all the array of loveliness, because it does not perceive it. What if it be so in spiritual matters—that it requires a radiance to be poured over a new scenery which has arisen in the field of view; and what were all the power of vision if that territory, which before lay away from all intellectual inspection, shrouded in obscurity, is not divested of the clouds and darkness which were suspended over it and were not irradiated with light, " as the bright shining of a candle giveth light"?

We are not unapprised of the leading theological tenet—that it is the Spirit which evolves out of the darkness this spiritual territory, and not only imparts a will to look in the direction of these things "that make for peace," but brings them out of their natural dimness and makes them clear in a flood of light which He pours over them. The light which is effused from the orb of day on the objects of vision is different from the organ which casts a glance in their direction. The organ which looks may not see for two reasons. First, because it is in a diseased state, and sees at best, as the man in the Gospel " saw men as walking trees." Secondly, it may not see them because, although in a sound state itself, the objects are in darkness. As long as it is a region of darkness and shadow of death the eye cannot see. If the landscape is to be seen, it must reflect its pencils of light on the sentient nerves of the visual organ. By means of light making the objects capable of being observed, a picture of them must be photographed on that delicate screen of network called the retina, stretched out at the back of the eye to receive them.

Nor is there a difference, whether the object to be seen be a celestial luminary floating in the canopy of heaven or au object in our own immediate vicinity. The interposing medium which renders all alike visible is light. Beams of light, emanating with inexpressible velocity from the sun, render him the object of vision. Beams of light, emanating from the earth and coming in contact with the organ destined to receive them, render them the objects of vision. In either case, "that which maketh manifest is light." To be seen, the indispensable condition is to be in the light. Objects have no power of bringing themselves within the sphere of vision. At night the eye is in as good order for discharging its functions as in day. But, instead of there being an interposing light, there is an interposing darkness, and this darkness itself absorbs the powers of vision. We might say that there is a beauty beyond the powers of mind to conceive, but it is a beauty in gloom. It is not discoverable. "No eye hath seen nor ear heard; nor hath it entered into the heart of man to conceive the things which God hath prepared for them that love Him." But to be seen they must be clear. To be discoverable they must be extricated from their obscurity.

These things here mainly shine forth in clearness of conception. The doctrine of an all-illuminating Spirit, who reveals new scenes to the mind, has little to do with those efforts by which the intellect of an expounder unfolds them to the mind. They are clear in so far as the earthly expositor makes them clear. By him they are brought within the sphere of individual consciousness. By him there is a sustained exhibition of them to the mind. By him the illustrations, appropriate to the due setting forth of the objects, are collected. He is thus actually the minister of God in eternal and unspeakable concerns. The Spirit has His province. The creature has his. And we learn from the teaching of inspiration that they are altogether compatible. If Paul plants, and Apollos waters, and God gives the increase, it is still the order of Divine economy that Paul should plant and Apollos water that which is planted. The Holy Spirit has not seen fit to occupy the place of these first heralds of the Gospel, but to use their talents; not to usurp their functions, but to impart a blessing to their efforts; not to supersede their labours by His own immediate and irresistible efficacy, but to render them so mighty as to be a blessing in the Messiah's kingdom.

If the Spirit represented these mysteries to the human mind, it would be, we conceive, by vivifying its conceptions of them. If man represents them, so as to give them power in conversion, he must try and show them to the human soul bathed in a flood of Divine effulgence. To bring them home to the heart; to educe them out of their concealment; to elucidate them so as to give outline and expression to them, is language which denotes nothing else but vividness of conception.

The object of preaching is, moreover, to affect the heart. And we hardly know which is the more difficult task, to represent Divine realities as that they shall assume an embodiment before the intellect, or that they shall actually impress the moral nature. Nor do we know that there is in every instance a connection between clearness of view and ardour of affection. Some, indeed, appear to possess just conceptions of the great things of faith. But their sympathies are as before. They are unmoved and unimpressed. Their affections are not enlisted in the cause. It would seem as if they were suddenly arrested on their onward progress to Christian perfection. They are half-finished Christians. Their intellects are enabled to portray the form of the temple; but they have not set their affections on things above, where Christ is seated "at the right hand of God."

Whether there may be a mode of conversion which only requires clearness in the intellect, without ardency of affections made alive and subdued by the views it has attained of the wonders of redemption, we cannot tell; but sure we are that ardour is generally understood as being a better mark of conversion than all the intellectual skill by which the great objects of faith can be rendered patent and observable.

It is, therefore, frequently found that where intellectual clearness fails, ardour, accompanied by none of this mental power, has succeeded. This has one explanation—that ardour actually declares that the speaker is what he is trying to make others; that he is himself "awaked out of sleep," "a new creature"; that old things have passed into oblivion, and all things have become new. He is presumed to possess the Spirit of Christ; while the other is presumed to be the man of fine scholarship, elegant taste, philosophical discernment. The one set of qualities makes us think that he has studied Christianity; that Christ has been to him a new teacher in the school of philosophy. The other quality makes us think that Christ has put His Spirit in him.

The object of the "preacher of righteousness" is to convince the sinner of his guilty and undone condition by nature, and that there is a "stronghold of hope," of which, if he lay hold, he shall be saved. "He that calleth on the name of the Lord shall be saved." It is to lead sinners to call on the name of the Lord. But how call on His name unless their calamity is seen to be so great as to induce them to do so. If the mariner be not seen to be in danger, he need not be anxious about keeping his vessel afloat; if he is in no peril, his perturbation is unreasonable.

It may require not only force of argument to make the hearer sensible of his danger, but require an ardour to carry into the heart the fear which must arise from a sense of danger. Intellectual pictures, without this energy, will not accomplish the object. The weeping of Christ over the thick-coming calamities of the devoted city showed the earnestness of His nature more than the description of the sins which drew down the Divine indignation. We may reasonably suppose that the minister who so beheld the tremendousness of spiritual death as to evince the beseeching ardour of one who really saw the magnitude of the calamity, as to pour forth the bitter tears of sorrow over the doom of the impenitent and unpardoned, would bear with a greater weight on spiritual intelligencies than one who, without this fervour, shed the light of fine intellectual faculties over the whole of his subject and pleased the intellectual.

Yet the truth is unmistakable, that the ardour of a mind wholly shut in by the narrow limits of a single thought would only induce contempt. It would be intolerable. It might be attended with an awakening effect by its vehemence; but, as a people become accustomed to such impetuosity, it would, without new modes of thought and expression, soon lose its power.

We are told of those who live near the heat and agitations of a volcano that the deluges of lava, which have blotted out so many vineyards and flowed over so many houses, are hardly cold when new houses arise on the same place. They know not when the mountain may again involve them in a new disaster. But they are not greatly alarmed at the mountain whose angry convulsions destroyed so many of their predecessors. They are used to it. They live in its din and uproar.

There is sometimes an energy associated with the still small voice which was not in the whirlwind and the earthquake.

The object of the Christian ambassador is not to make an intellectual demonstration, but produce a spiritual result. It might be affirmed that it was more to produce a moral than an intellectual result. Thus moral, more than intellectual, means may be demanded. Were so many individuals, equipped with

the finest powers of intellect, to engage in the business of
converting the human soul to God, they might be far surpassed
by the men of ardour who were saved themselves, and had
experienced the magnitude of the peril, and performed themselves all the steps of the mighty process. With the one class
the matter is an intellectual gratification; with the other it is
an experience. And as men are ardent from conviction, and not
from mere intellect, so it would seem that, in the grand work of
conversion, the mightiest weapon is vehemence, and the
mightiest instrument is he who has himself come through the
conflict.

But the man of ardour ought not to hold in contempt the
man of intellect or his studies. Both owe their respective
qualities and tendencies to Another. They are not their own.
If they occasionally made the effort to enter into one another's
domain; if conception created ardour, and outburst was more
founded on intellect, the pulpit, thus furnished and blessed with
such workmen, would acquire a glory and a power before an un-
believing world far beyond the most sanguine expectations.

CHAPTER III.

SUBJECTS NATURALLY SUITED TO THE PULPIT.

WE now proceed to consider the themes which the pulpit employs, and which, by the right use of them, may be supposed to be fraught with interest to those who hear. In the foregoing remarks it has been our endeavour to show that there are obstacles in the way of a minister's efficiency with which, as he can never overcome them, he has little to do. The Scriptures suppose the subjects to be distasteful. "To the natural man" they are foolishness. Fashion has now given these doctrines an importance, and hearers can comply with the exactions of this fickle deity without any more ado than appearing in the house of prayer on the Sabbath. Like the Athenians, crowds no longer press tumultuously along to enjoy the sensation of something new, or to be gratified with the logical cleverness of refuting it. Though stamped with the venerable grandeur of antiquity, yet the Gospel story is now allowed to enjoy an obsolete senility. Its claims are granted, and it is permitted the honours of an old age which has seen good service and witnessed exciting exploits. Like the aged warrior, it is allowed to talk of its achievements and still to labour under the serious conviction that it can only console itself with its ancient reminiscences, believing that the fire of its former ardour is extinct.

But is it satisfied with this consolation? As a Divine system, does Christianity suffer the langour or debility of age? Is not its motto that of its most honoured ambassador, "forgetting the things which are behind, and pressing forward to those which are before"? Would it not willingly exchange the recollection of a hoary antiquity for the positive performance of some exploits in our own day—for putting to flight some ghastly and cruel phantom of ignorance, and bringing to the foot of the cross the lofty imaginations of men? And what is there to forbid to the ministry of the Word the rejoicing anticipation that great triumphs are still in store for the Christian system? What is there which can warrant their settling down into an ignoble repose, as if mankind had assumed a stereotyped condition, utterly impenetrable to the most fervent and importunate appeals that can be made?

If Christianity possessed nothing more than the grandeur of the subjects over which she expatiates; if she sat disconsolate, and yet with the names God, Eternity, Repentance, Faith engraven on her forehead, we would not despair with regard to the prospects of her futurity. Subjects like these wax not old, because they are not only impressed on the page of Revelation, but indelibly traced on the human soul. Some words possess in themselves, independently of association with any system, a spirit which awakens an echo and sympathy in the human bosom. They cause a chord to vibrate; they ring among the recesses of our thoughts; they awaken to interests sublime and absorbing; they appear to be a part of a nature which existed long before them. As if they had been breathed in paradise, there is something on their mere utterance which moves in unison with them when we hear them. Like grammar, which must exist incorporated in language, so these words seem to exist interwoven with the essence of human souls. The intellect of man excogitates such words. Revelation does not impart to him that part of his nature in virtue of which his soul throbs in harmony with them. They exercise a spell on him in a state altogether unenlightened, as with a touch from above. And if Revelation can wield them in unison with other subjects, she is then most likely to attract attention for those other enunciations which are peculiar to the volume of her disclosures.

Space and eternity were assumed by Dr. Samuel Clarke to be two attributes, the simple conception of which should, according to him, have satisfied conscience with regard to the Divine existence. "If they were attributes," said he, "they must be attributes of something, and that something must be God." Would it not have been better if he had said that man's felt delight in the word eternity was a kind of presumption that he was meant to inhabit it? More good would have been done by such a practical application.

Of all the expressions calculated to affect the soul, perhaps the word eternity is the most powerful. An endless procession of ages, a projection of time in its continuous flux, is like some imaginary river which flows into no ocean, but whose stream is itself endless. A few hundred years are, on the page of our earthly history, sufficient to constitute an eternity here. The uneducated intellect exhausts itself in the attempt to carry the burden of two or three centuries. Of far-distant times it can form no adequate conception. The cycles of geology baffle all its calculations. It cannot figure to itself a series of far-receding ages, at the beginning of whose ascending march along the stream of time, we might say, stands the Mosaic account of creation, stretching far away into the distant past. Nor can the intellect of the most nobly gifted of our species add age to age so as to form to itself an idea of such vastness. Let a grain of sand be every century removed from our world. We suppose that an eternity would be spent when the last grain of sand would be removed. But just as many centuries would have passed as there are grains in the composition of our globe. What, however, is this world to the system of which it constitutes a member, or to those luminaries suspended in the immensity around it? The endless progression of centuries would not be at all arrested by such an undertaking. It would remain interminable as before. Nor, if placed at the last term in such a series, should we have any other feeling but that eternity was before us still in all its incomprehensible vastness, exceeding our every effort to grasp or to confine such immensity in the limits of thought—a thing to amaze, to bewilder, to overwhelm!

There is, besides, the grand consideration that One inhabits that eternity and pervades it with the ubiquity of His life-giving presence. Before Him it is one eternal NOW, not to Him, perhaps, distinguishable by a succession of moments, as it is to man's feeble conceptions—a duration over which He may cast His glance, and whose amplitude may all be submitted to His Divine inspection. That there is a Being to whose nature it may pertain to take this infinitude into view, as it belongs to us to behold the occurrences of a moment, is equally wonderful with the endlessness of the duration. A thousand years may be in His sight as one day. So wonderful is His essence, so astonishing His nature, that events in our view, separated by the wide interval of millenniums, may to the All-seeing Eye be quite contemporaneous. Man's ephemeral and contracted existence, his days "few and evil," bear no appreciable proportion to this amazing duration. Expand into an age every one of our moments, swell every little interval of time into a period as large as has elapsed since the creation of the world, and we have a longevity which we have no means of measuring. Yet is there a beginning and an expiration of that duration. Add millions of these periods, have we gained a commensurate conception of what we designate as eternity? When our lives are projected into another state of being, and millions of years have passed away in jubilations and praises, will it be any sensible reduction of the infinite endlessness, or will we feel as if we had journeyed some way along the ever-lengthening vista and are nearer to its end?

But what frustrates our every effort at summoning into existence an adequate idea of this eternity is that it has no end. If we have got successfully to the close of one series, we are as far off the attainment of our object as before. Dealing with a duration that is boundless, we are seeking to put limits to it. We are trying to confine infinity in the limits of our contracted and shortcoming fancies. Let the calculus of earth measure the cycles and periods of creation. This is its function. But this growing and ever-increasing and never-ending duration far surpasses our terrestrial arithmetic, and casts a mockery on the loftiest effort of intellect to compress it within the littleness of earthly periods or measure it by the paltryness of earthly applications.

But another subject frequently met with in the eloquence of the pulpit, though without the general effect which the above-mentioned theme has naturally on the soul of man, is what is called Faith. However it may be reduced more to the standard of human thought, more to the understanding of sensitive beings, understood in its theological sense, it is that by which man as a sinner is justified, not as the efficient cause of his justification, but because it is the identical attitude which the creature must assume to the ground of his justification, which

c

is the righteousness of Christ; and instead of saying we are justified by the righteousness of Christ, we say we are "justified by faith." Indeed, the expression, "justification by faith," has of late assumed more the position of a mere theological formulary of great importance in creeds and confessions. And certainly those who could so illustrate it, and eliminate it, and expound it, as to bring it in some way within the sympathies and experience of ordinary persons, would be worthy of great acknowledgments from the Church of God.

Articles are too formal either to contain themselves or to impart much life to others. They are by many minds regarded as austerities, if not barbarities of thought, worthy of the times when to pass some fiery ordeal was a triumphant refutation of the most odious charges. Though indispensable, they yet are charged with the imputation of fettering human thought, challenging it on its devious excursions into the land of unsubstantial speculation, demanding of it the right it has to be off the legitimate ground of established opinion, and dismissing it back again to the path from which it had made its heretical deviation.

To humanize faith, to disentangle it from the elements of that theology of which many entertain the idea that it is a system which does not interfere nor at all busy itself with humanity, we might say of it that the word does not mean anything esoteric, anything which the initiated alone can understand. It means confidence, reliance, trust. We do not consider it as meaning an inward feeling altogether undefinable. We cannot sympathize with those who would give to the word in Divine and supernatural systems a meaning it has not in human systems. We cannot understand those who say that it is a name altogether by itself, and which no other vocable can represent. If there be dependence on a mere man that he will scrupulously adhere to his word, or make good what he has promised, this is faith in him. If there be dependence on Christ, or the efficacy of His sacrifice, or the peace-procuring power of His blood, or the prevalence of His intercession, or the truth of His promises, this is faith in Him. That principle or state of the soul is the same whatever be the object before it. It may be confidence in the good-will of a friend, or his ability or his fidelity. In that case the object before our view is the friend whose general kindness has produced that effect.

It will be easily seen that this view of the subject does not interfere with the operation of the Spirit in creating faith in the soul. Though faith were allowed to be the exercise of the mental faculties, with some particular object before them, it may still be "the gift of God." It is to be presumed that where faith is spoken of, it is implied that there are beings who are possessed of it or who exercise it. If this were not the case, how could we appreciate the advantage of the term at all? It has a real existence. What, then, we would ask, would be the explanation of one who, instead of making faith the subject of his conversation, possessed it himself; who, betaking himself to a view of his spiritual experience, could declare that he had faith in Christ? Do we suppose he would make his faith inexplicable or mysterious, or would he say he felt he was a sinner and had faith in the atonement which Christ, as his surety, had made for his sins? Would it be anything more than a case of fiducial dependence upon the power of Christ?

The grand object of this spiritual trust, however, is the righteousness of Christ, as the great federal head of His people, and their consequent righteousness in Him. They are accounted as possessed of a righteousness, because faith unites them with Christ. Never, by their mightiest efforts, could they become righteous in themselves, or satisfy the offended majesty of Heaven's law, which demanded either their punishment or perfect obedience. It demanded obedience without a flaw. Anything else would be injurious to God's prerogative—would be an insult to His majesty. But what they cannot do for themselves Christ has done for them. They have every possible warrant, while they cannot put faith in their own merits, to put faith in the righteousness of Another. Coming to Him with the conviction of their own inability to magnify the law, they are directed to have faith in Christ as so doing. By so doing they honour Christ, and God regards them as entitled to the benefit of His sufferings and death.

But this faith is opposed to any right or title we could establish to the Divine favour by any righteousness which belongs to man, because of a rectitude which never swerved from the straight line of strict justice, or of amiable virtues by which his character was adorned, or by wide and thoughtful benevolence. Our virtues carry in them such a mixture of selfishness, weakness, constitutional tendency; so little do they rise from the single principle of the Divine glory, that though they may be possessed of high and, we trust, useful qualities, they are not able to compensate for general depravity, or counteract habitual transgression, or engage the regards of Heaven. We detract not from the loveliness of natural virtues. They form the most beauteous exhibition man can make in this world; and, even when strengthened and directed by Divine grace, are scarce distinguishable from what they were in a state of nature. We only maintain that natural virtue has its proper place and admiration; that it is not by any means our reconcilement to Heaven. We place a loftier virtue, by far, in that station of mediatory eminence, and that is the virtue of the death and atonement of Christ. We ask for it an estimation in the human soul which cannot be awarded to anything terrestrial. Our view of the unspotted holiness of God's law, of the shrinking sanctity of His everlasting kingdom, compels us to connect our title to heaven, not with obedience of our own, but obedience of Him who brought in everlasting righteousness.

When man has faith in this righteousness it becomes his, for it is received by faith; and it is evident that instead of injuring the interests of vital godliness, this faith, where it is real, must operate in advancing its interests. This will be apparent if it be considered what holiness is. It is not so much an act as it is a quality—a fixed habit of the soul, determined on conformity with the Divine commandments. It is a life above the world, and greatly above its habits and customs. Made holy, the soul is under a perpetual alarm for fear of offence—"That I may not sin against Thee." It becomes sensitively delicate about what would induce reprehension or involve contamination. And surely faith in Christ is a state of the soul with which sin, in its power and excess and unhallowed impiety, is utterly incompatible! If any asserted the possibility of faith in Christ as our righteousness subsisting at the same time with unbridled profligacy or wanton profanity, they then make Christ the minister of sin. Because the meritorious righteousness on which they found their acceptance before God is Christ's, it does not follow that they may discard the righteousness of personal holiness which the Spirit creates; and when we consider from the filial relationship to God, which they have assumed, under what serious obligations they are placed to show forth a family resemblance by which, even in this world, they may be recognized as His children, we cannot but see that it would be a spurious faith which led to sin, an evangelical and substantial faith which led to holiness.

It may be observed that those themes which rather pertain to Natural Theology, or which may be illustrated in a manner in which its subjects are illustrated, possess more interest for most people than those which are altogether theological or merely systematic. There is something in the one, from their nature, fitted to create sympathy—to break the olden lethargy, and awaken to high and immortal interests. What is merely peculiar to a system may be treated in a manner which, from taste or invention in the speaker, may create attention, while what touches on some passion, feeling or tendency in human nature must beget emotion. Thus the office, work and attributes of the Spirit may be wrought into some beautiful intellectual system. But if, at the same time, we do not understand how such a system is fitted to affect the heart, we have created no more interest than what is common to those who delight in controversial discussion, in balancing the merits of different systems, or pleasing their intellect by the invention and canvassing of new ideas. If philosophy was the better of being recalled from its theories and dogmata, the sooner theology is arranged to answer the tendencies and constitution of the human mind the more expectation will we have of a real and not a chimerical usefulness.

Perhaps none of the topics which the Christian teacher can select for the purpose of affecting is attended with that power of raising the emotions, and leading to serious reflection, as what Dr. Chalmers was accustomed to term "the tremendous necessity." The ways in which it makes its insidious approaches are so many, the circumstances of its appearance are so various, the process so inevitable, the destinies it decides so momentous and unchanging, that we know not if any subject can be made so effectual in answering the end of preaching, which is generally supposed to consist in affecting rather than informing. To bid adieu to everything viewed here in the most pleasing light, and connected with our purest associations; to let go our hold of the living and substantial world—its companies, its enjoyments, and the witchery of its varied fascinations, and to sink into loathsomeness and putrefaction; to pass into a state in which the changes and passions of earth no more excite and no more annoy; why, before a step so momentous would cease to interest and alarm, we must have got rid of feelings and tendencies which make us what we are.

Yet the view which is frequently given of death—unmitigated, too, by any of those arguments which have influence with a reasoning mind in producing reconcilement to its infliction—is one which rather tends to a total thoughtlessness or entire acquiescence. This may be considerably modified by actually contemplating the spectacle of a death-bed—inspecting, if we might so speak, its phenomena—considering its various stages, from debility to fainting sickness, to unconsciousness, to departure. In speaking of the obscurity and darkness which spread themselves over man's life, a divine, celebrated as well for his eloquence as his farsighted sagacity, observes, "The mystery is tenfold aggravated by the thousand ills which are scattered along the journey of human life, and, above all, by its appalling termination in the agonies, and the cruel separations, and the dark and revolting hideousness of death."

Abundant argument is found in the Gospel for mitigating the sorrows of departure. The eye of faith is directed to Him who has, in a great measure, disarmed the last and dreadful enemy of his terror. Yet what may be the precise amount of these consolations in the case of the dying, how they may then be remembered or may affect them, whether the terrible ordeal is not such as deprives them of all power of thought, is a matter concerning which our little knowledge forbids us pronouncing a decided opinion. Death is so very similar, not only in all grades, but in all characters, that it scarcely presents any variety save that of excruciating agony, delirium or repose. We have certainly heard of those of known piety and acknowledged usefulness suffering in their last moments unspeakable agony, yet the agony of "heirs of salvation."

To counteract the natural horrors of death by any arguments but those purely evangelical, or which are derived from faith, is an effort which is never successful. The Christian is far more useful here than the Natural Theology. It has been attempted, but we are not certain whether any effort would not be attended with more success. The butterfly, soaring away into fields of air, and sunning its beauty in the beams of solar splendour, leaving behind it the earthly *involucrum* in which it was imprisoned, is presented in the analogies of philosophy as an instance of actual resurrection—at least as a instance somewhat similar to what the body passes through in the grave. However, the analogy is so very loose as to be almost useless. None could be deceived by it but the most superficial observers. There is nothing in the case of this painted child of air at all analogous to the resurrection. And yet nothing is more frequently employed as a natural argument to reconcile man to the severity of departure—to the hideousness of death.

Another analogy by which to illustrate the resurrection, and render the approach of death less alarming, is the celebrated one of the Apostle, when he mentions the "bare grain" imbedded in the soil, and God imparting a body to it as it pleases Him. Some have, unwarrantably enough, endeavoured to follow out the analogy further than the modesty of Paul has permitted him. Deeming that some minute particle in the seed is the germ of the future ear or tree, and that it is actuated at the proper season by strange movements, and expands and sends out its pedicles and verdure, they have made the human fabric describe the same process. As a seed, it must be planted in the grave. It must evanish into the noisomeness of decay. It must be resolved into its primitive elements. But there is in it, they say, a germ which passes safe through all these transitions. The grave cannot touch that small particle, which preserves itself amid the general putrescency. Small as the atom is, imperceptible to human view as it is, evasive as it is of all efforts to pursue it to the favoured receptacle it has honoured with its presence, yet it is mighty enough to resist the encroachments of dissolution all around it.

But as the argument on this subject derives so little from anything taken from the field of natural illustration, it will be found that nothing so repels the imagination of gloom and decay as the fine prospect of life everlasting rising into view beyond death and the grave. Immortality, anticipated by Christian faith, must be the grand antidote of the dismalness of the sepulchre. By faith it can be said that we are going to "the land of uprightness." It is no more than a journey, the outset of which is, it is true, attended by the "horror of a great darkness," the first step of which is the most terrible; but as we advance a celestial air breathes delight, and a heavenly panorama rises on the astonished vision. The light which shines in that wondrous region far exceeds the light of the sun. The people who inhabit that glorious land are a holy people, their hearts and exercises in perfect harmony; and while here the thoughts of the worshipper are carried away into a thousand devious wanderings, the sport of every bright and transient delusion, there one great object of worship unites all their praises. For Him they tune the harp. At His feet they cast the crown. He is the never-ceasing prompter of their devotions and their anthems. Earth has no scene of such rare, dazzling, varied beauty which can enter into competition with the celestial purity and glory of that place where "His servants serve Him."

Nothing more is required to loose the bands of death, and deprive him of his sting, than the exhibition of life. It thus becomes the portal of life. A moment's darkness, and then light, which is here "inaccessible and full of glory!" A disappearance from one region, and entrance on another of unspeakable splendour! A brief night of the tomb, and a dawn of radiancy which no eye hath seen! A convulsion and an icy coldness, succeeded by the beamy warmth of immortal glory! Such representations as these are, we conceive, not only useful as declaring Gospel facts, but as fitted to comfort and impress. The grandeur of immortality is an idea naturally calculated to create those very emotions which melt the heart and fit it for the reception of the Gospel. The soul assumes a fortitude from this truth which does not by nature belong to it; and thus that ordeal, which solemnizes the gay, terrifies the courageous, and sobers the thoughtless, may have such a brilliancy cast around it as, while it prompts our piety, quiets the tremors of nature sinking into decay.

Another topic, capable of 'descriptive illustration to any extent, and fitted to create emotions of awe and alarm, is that which was a good deal dwelt upon by ancient preachers and writers, but is now not near so much adverted to as it ought— I mean that awful array, those awards and convictions after death, generally brought before our notice by the expression, "the judgment." "After death the judgment." The human mind seems to be desirous to deliver itself from the influence of truths which might be thought to be mechanical or factitious, which cannot be founded on or illustrated by some department of visible nature. And forasmuch as it is supposed to be quite too mechanical to suppose Him who knows the recondite privacies of all souls to assume the office of a judge, or set up a court of distributive justice, or issue the writs for the appearance of those to be tried, and in solemn state, amid the most alarming convulsions of nature or spectacles of sublimity, to listen to the sentence, they have alleged that it would be unbecoming the majesty of Heaven, or inconsistent with Omniscience, to make this investigation by means of witnesses, or dismiss one party into the abodes of despair, while the other hears the sentence which ushers them into glory.

But those who look on all these preparations as unnecessary, from the nature of the Divine Being, cannot deny that though the whole were only metaphor, yet the development of these descriptions in the Bible, by all the accompaniments of a court of judicature, such as the sound of trumpet and approach of prisoners for trial, would be fitted in a high degree to accomplish the end in view—even to melt and subdue the human soul, and produce alarm about the most momentous of its interests. How it shall appear before its Maker, whom it may have incensed by its neglect; how it shall meet the scrutiny of His gaze or the indignation of His frown; what shall be the shield of its protection at that awful moment; how, if not made meet for heaven, it is not meet to confront its Judge; these are enquiries which derive their power from such a description as we have adverted to.

There is really nothing about which any great scrupulousness may be entertained, as though we were describing something that never took place. Of its propriety or likelihood in the system of the universe, we are at best but judges inadequately informed. We cannot pronounce on what is fitting or inconsistent in God to accomplish. To give a signal rebuke to wickedness, as well as to reward fidelity, God, for aught we know to the contrary, may set up a judicatory, and bring to view some universal standard of judgment. It is not for us, as if we knew all, to pronounce on what is becoming or is unbecoming either the goodness or justice of Him "who sitteth on the throne." If the all-knowing Spirit has thought fit to represent this general judgment as a theme which, for its grandeur, might become an auxiliary in the preacher's hand in the business of conversion, there can be nothing improper in the minister of Jesus Christ making use of it, and presenting it with all the accompaniments of terror and majesty which may comfort or may alarm.

There are many other subjects which may properly be introduced to the attention of an auditory—as the fall, sin, repentance, adoption, faith, holiness, with innumerable moral topics, which the preacher will be far astray if he neglect, under the impression that he is going beyond the evangelical precincts, and becoming a preacher of mere morality. Why pride, calumny, envy, censoriousness, benevolence, charity, courtesy, loyalty, and similar subjects, should be excluded from the pulpit, is a circumstance which they, perhaps, can explain best whose ideas are attached to some familiar round from which they cannot deliver themselves. Indeed, whatever may deserve censure in the fashions of society or the conduct of human beings is not deserving of contempt or oversight. If the exacting can be made merciful, "the churl bountiful," the penurious liberal, the falsely proud made to see that all are subject to the same accidents, and differ only in a few circumstantials, surely it is not the spirit of the Gospel to hold these amendments in disregard or aversion! We admit that to preach the Gospel is to preach Christ as the only foundation of a sinner's hope; not, we presume, to preach a mere name, but to describe the features of His likeness, and try and engrave them on men's souls. The atonement ought to be the grand subject of most discourses. But a wise man will consider how he will best elevate the thoughts, enlarge the soul, and give it the impulse of high and generous emotions. And he will be sure, while doing so, that he is giving a development to emotions of the soul which may lead it the more readily to have faith in the self-sacrificing character of that Divine love which, stooping from heaven, has bowed itself to the earth to die and to redeem.

CHAPTER IV.

TEXTS.

EVERY sermon is presumed to take its character and pro-portions from words prefixed to it. These words form the text, and contain some doctrine or suggest some subject, the treatment of which may be acceptable or may be attended with profit. It is not essential that there be a very close connection between the words which form the text and the sermon which flows from them. A preacher may be too textual. However, it is requisite that they be not opposed. Thus, were a sermon to be preached from such words as these, "And Abraham stood up, and bowed himself to the people of the land, even to the children of Heth" (Gen. xxiii. 7), we do not suppose that from them the preacher would inculcate a lesson of humility, but of courtesy. They present to the mind a picture of the stately and ceremonious politeness of oriental kingdoms. Again, it is pre-sumed that the virtue of generosity is not what would be deduced from such a text as this, "And let fall also some of the handfuls on purpose for her, and leave them, that she may glean them, and rebuke her not" (Ruth ii. 16). It would be the delicate attentions of genuine charity, seeking to convey its offering without offend-ing the sensibilities of the recipient.

As it is reprehensible to treat any portion of Scripture with flippancy, so it is a reproach to the dignity of the pulpit to affect singularity. We hope that the stories are untrue which inform us of one minister, that he selected for his text an "Oh"; of another, that "If" became the motto of his discourse; and of a third, that his exuberance of fancy enabled him to preach from the word "But." Such attempts are to be looked upon as puer-ilities worthy of the wit of a schoolboy and the condemnation of a Christian.*

---

*An elder, who was something of a wit himself, had listened to a sermon which a young aspirant preached on the word "But." After the service he had an opportunity of speaking to the young preacher, and his criticism, so unfavourable, was thus expressed:—"A good smart sermon; 'but' you will not do for this congregation." But the discourse might be favourably received elsewhere.

It ought to be kept in mind that the pulpit loses its dignity in the eyes of the intelligent when it is made the scene of any indecorous exhibition or trifling of this nature. It is the stage where they take their stand, who are looked upon as ambassadors, fraught with tidings and counsels from the court of Heaven. The treasure has been deposited in earthen vessels. The trust has been committed to these vessels, not that the message delivered by them may be imbued with any taint of earthliness, but that the excellency of the whole may be seen to be of God. If He condescend to honour these earthen receivers by making them so many depositories of Divine truth, or so many lights in the world, it is not for them to come forward with the playful conceits of fancy or the sallies of unsanctified wit. It is for them, if there be any temptation from peculiar tendencies, to repress them as far as possible, and choose such texts as shall conduct to other subjects, and so to mortify, as it were, the promptings of an unholy inventiveness. Who was ever improved by Sterne's sermon on the advice of the wise man—"It is better to go to the house of mourning, than to go to the house of feasting" (Eccles. vii. 2)? He commences it with the exclamation, "I deny that." It is not going too far to say of that sermon, that instead of attracting the Christian to it for consolation it has repelled him; and that, while the salutary direction is forgotten, this petty witticism of his exordium is all that has carried it down to posterity. Indeed, while the ingenuity of Sterne was fitted to give very pleasing turns to his discourses, and while the latter abound with paragraphs which are models of correct composition, we are afraid that where the character of his tendencies and play of his fancy in his other works are known, his sermons, however well composed, can hardly be perused with much pleasure or with much benefit.

Texts, in general, ought to be selected, according as they present some universal truth to the mind, which may give opportunity for adorning it with illustrations, and may exercise to some degree the abilities of the writer. This is what Cicero styles the *universum genus*, on which eloquence has made its finest displays. There is room here for imagery and expansion to any extent. A mind of average ability will feel at ease in expatiating on subjects of this order. We have reason to believe that the hearers enjoy the same experience. The mind may, in general, discover something new on a subject, where it is left greatly to its own cogitations, and where such a broad expanse is disclosed before it. Historical portraitures will not recommend themselves unless in connection with some abstract quality by which they are distinguished. Thus the meekness of Moses, the patience of Job, the holy fortitude of Daniel. The mere personage cannot delight, attended with a dry catalogue of the actions he has performed or the words he has spoken. It requires a quality to command attention. Actions cannot be appropriated. They belong to circumstance, age, and temper. The person may be imitated in his forbearance, temperance, charity. Some leading feature, therefore, amplified and diversified, according to its nature, may be attended with this advantage; that it may, when exhibited in features either engaging or repulsive, allure by its beauties, or deter by its deformity.

But inasmuch as the Divine volume is, if not wholly, at least principally, intended to reveal the condescension and love of the universal Father for the children who have withdrawn their allegiance from Him, the subject which has the most claim on the preacher's powers is "the love of God which passeth understanding." Nor let it be imagined that this topic has received an exhaustive illustration in the exercises of the pulpit. It admits of almost endless treatment, from the number of subjects which lie in its vicinity. There is "the goodness of God, which leadeth to repentance." There is His benevolence, which will not have the sinner to perish. There is the providence of God, which clothes the grass of the field, and on which his dependence is to be placed that it will clothe him. And there is the all-absorbing love of God, "who so loved the world as to give His Son, that whosoever believeth on Him should not perish, but might have everlasting life." And there is the essence of God, where it says, "God is love." Like to some beauteous crystallization, this love of God may send out from its grand centre of redeeming love and good-will those minor formations or veins of love and attention in the kingdom of nature and providence, and thus stir souls up not to forget Him and His benefits.

The student of the Bible will find a most ample field in his pious efforts for constructing monuments to the Divine goodness, and Divine qualities in general, from almost every one of its pages. Nor are those passages in vain which inform us of God being "a consuming fire"; of His "wrath burning as an oven"; and His "fury being poured out." As in His general economy, no doubt, these severer attributes of His nature are manifested for the "terror of the evil-doer." Thus the Apostle declares, He "will render to every man according to his deeds; to them who, by patient continuance in well-doing, seek for glory, honour, and immortality, eternal life; but unto them that are contentious, and do not obey the truth, but obey unrighteousness, indignation and wrath." There is a tendency, no. doubt, to soften and subdue those severer features of the Godhead and give a prominence to more attractive qualities—to present such an exhibition of Him as may engage rather than repel—perhaps to merge His whole economy into general and undistinguishing benevolence.

But the question is not so much of what exact attributes the Divine nature consists, as what aspects of that nature it may be most desirable to illustrate for the purpose of adding to the kingdom of Christ. We know what was the character of the admonitions, rebukes, warnings, and denunciations employed by Christ Himself. It cannot be out of the way to represent qualities which may inspire awe as well as prompt affection, which may command respect as well as subdue by tenderness.

In one great aspect of His nature, God may be viewed as the offended Governor, whose majesty has been insulted and His statutes infringed, and who might feel within Him all the impulse of a wrath which would wholly destroy and bring to nought a generation of evil-doers who have rebelled against Him. It is right to regard the Searcher of Hearts as actuated by an impetuous abhorrence of sin, as well as being moved with the yearnings of a strong compassion towards His disobedient and unhappy family. We do not sympathize with any treatment which might obliterate any feature of the Divinity. He is true to His denunciations, as He is to His promises. His wrathful announcements have their use in His grand economy. There is "the thunder of His power," as well as the sunshine of His favour. He allures by His smile, as well as terrifies by His frown. And by the skilful development and blending of such qualities, it is likely that hearts may be affected and the number of true disciples increased.

The end and use of sermons might be reduced to three objects—pathos, instruction, and improvement. It is the aim of the exercises of the pulpit to affect, instruct, amend. If these be not duly kept before the mind and, to some extent, made to pervade the discourse, it may be plainly seen that the minister who has delivered it had not kept sufficiently in view, on that occasion, the meaning of his office or its understood agency in the conversion of souls.

It might be, perhaps, affirmed that texts which move are more useful than those which only instruct. Every hearer may be presumed to be possessed of a moral rather than an intellectual nature. We do not undervalue powers of mind that can exercise their acumen on the wide domain of universal truth and estimate the force of evidence. But there ought to be, in general, in a text something which can be expanded into a power to take hold of the sinner and shake him out of his lethargy, which might demolish the strongholds of sinful habit and give him no repose in a fatal security. A text ought to be found wherewith to accomplish this, in which the sacred orator may, as it were, from consecrated ground, pour his burning thoughts over a mighty multitude. This warmth will melt when nothing else will. This will beat down and reduce that might of resistance—or worse than might of resistance—that might of indifference, compared with the strength of which the forthputting of the highest effort is too frequently found to be but little more than the lispings of infancy.

A text of this description may be a centre from which all the blandness of persuasion, terrors of denunciation, and vehemence of entreaty may be made to bear on an assembled multitude. And it strikingly agrees with what has been said, that the sacred record abounds with such texts. Everywhere, in fitting and urgent terms, sinners are entreated to hear and obey the Divine call. The fervent declamation of Moses and the prophets was directed to this object. "Now therefore, if ye will obey my voice indeed, and keep my covenant, then ye shall be a peculiar treasure unto me above all people" (Exod. xix. 5).

But this pathos has to do with more than the urgency of persuasion. It contains ideas of angry denunciation, entreaty, warning. It has to produce such emotions as good-will, gratitude, affection, fear, reverence. Into as many distinct forms of emotion as the moral interior is divided, so many kinds of texts may be discovered, which may furnish a groundwork on which the sacred assailant may take his stand, and from which he may discharge volley after volley, till the stubborn front of opposition be beaten down and a breach made for the entrance of the King. The youthful preacher ought to arrange a body of texts in methodical order, leaving it to time, circumstance and feeling, to point to the one which he wanted.

But one end of preaching is also to "instruct the ignorant." Texts must be looked for, which may be made convenient channels along which to convey information. This implies elucidation, development, precision. There may occasionally be a truth which, from general laxity, or want of care, from the attacks of a hostile party, or idea of its great importance, it may be needful to present in a light clearer than what has yet shone upon it. It has been said that the Bible is a book which a child may peruse, but which contains truths the highest intellects may not fathom. Coming from within a mysterious enclosure, which stands so far apart from the human or natural, it must possess difficult and recondite mysteries, which it is still legiti-mate for the mind to examine, unfold, and bring out to view, with the mystery brought into reconcilement with the clearness and obviousness which rest on some provinces of nature and Providence. Christ proposed to show to His disciples "the mysteries of the kingdom of heaven," and He presented them in parables, which it was their business to interpret by the powers of attention and reflection until, in the exercise, light was elicited and evolved on their understanding. Some texts may be selected before others, as containing subjects which the preacher may attempt to elucidate. The mysteries of the Sonship, Trinity, or Incarnation, rather than Election, may be given as instances.

D

Texts which convey information will generally state some proposition, which may be expanded; such as, "God is merciful," or "Our God is one Lord," or "God is love," or "The fear of the Lord is the beginning of wisdom," or "He that doeth the will of God, he shall know of the doctrines, whether they be of God." When a general statement is made, the mind of the hearer can be interested by illustrations and divisions of the subject.

The fact of the necessity of such texts arises from the necessity of addressing Christians of different degrees of knowledge and intelligence. In a large collection of people, there cannot but be some who are opposed to the transports of a zeal which they cannot understand, and who are pleased with fine distinctions and logical deductions. Texts which lead to the intellectual discussion of subjects, by which their thoughts may have been perplexed or occupied ; to the statement of objections, and their distinct refutation, are their delight; and, as there is nothing wrong or inconsistent in such demands, so in gratifying them in a moderate degree, and in selecting the verse or passage which admits this mode of treatment, there can be nothing which requires condemnation.

It must be remembered that the articles of faith, as they stand drawn up in creeds and confessions, will give rise to a number of texts giving abundant exercise to the intellect. The truths proposed will be stated in distinct propositions. The verses of Scripture intended to prove these propositions will take the form of propositions themselves. And the preacher, if he finds himself possessed of controversial ability, or that his tastes lie in this direction, will be profitably employed in elucidating, evincing, and demonstrating truths supposed to form the basis of Christianity.

The verse or portion of Scripture prefixed to a discourse may also be intended to improve or reform, or may be the vehicle of a command; as, "Abstain from all appearance of evil," "The will of God is your sanctification," "Be ye clean," "Put on charity," "Cease to do evil; learn to do well." Texts of this kind also abound in the inspired volume. It is of consequence, therefore, that in the preparations of the pulpit they also find a place. The great object of such passages is, doubtless, to

revolutionize, change, transform, convert; to act on the sentiments and affections, and hence on the conduct and history.
When a "minister of the sanctuary" enters on the enforcement
or explanation of the prescription, "Be ye perfect, as your Father
which is in heaven is perfect," the object is not only to inculcate
and explain Christian perfection, but to make the hearers each
an embodiment of the virtue which is prescribed. The text
enforces a Christian virtue. The heart is such that it can be
moulded into the form of that virtue; and the object certainly
is, by explanation, illustration and earnestness, to produce the
virtue itself.

Is any hearer found to be addicted to the sin of censoriousness? there is a text in which this sin may be explained and, if
possible, eradicated. Is another inclined to the sin of self-
esteem, which regards all others as inferiors? this quality may,
by means of a fitting text, be shown in its nature, unreasonable-
ness and odiousness. Is envy the dominant habit with another?
its hatefulness and removal may be shown and attempted from
some utterance of the Bible. Is avarice the quality which de-
forms the character of another? Achan, who lost his soul by
this vice, may give a warning by which it may be represented,
and its hateful nature and calamitous results be presented. Do
the rewards of ambition immoderately fascinate and intoxicate
the soul, so that it no longer perceives the law of its God? the
volume of the book will no doubt furnish vocables by which the
folly and absorbing nature of this vice may be described.

In general, a text ought to be selected in proportion to its
decided bearing on some particular doctrine or subject. And it
would not be wholly unadvisable if the preacher first selected a
subject for illustration, and betook himself to the Bible to discover
a text which suited it. Thus, were it calumny or the claims of
truth, Providence or fidelity, which he wished to describe or
enforce, he possesses in his mind the general idea before he has
found the verses of Scripture from which he will exhibit his subject
in its nature or consequences, whether pernicious or useful.
This must be the case when the sermon is delivered for the
occasion ; such as the death of an eminent character. Then it
is that the man of taste is found to be possessed of acknowledged

superiority in point of judgment. His text is seen to be the one out of Revelation best fitted to the mournful occasion; and it is not unlikely that his treatment of his subject will display discrimination and eloquence.

Though all Scripture presents abundant material to serve the purposes of persuasion and instruction, yet, as two or three thousand verses would be enough for the longest and most laborious lifetime, it is necessary to make the verses which suggest a subject as telling and decided as posible. The Bible is not such a book as that the very first passage which would offer itself to an eye directed to its verses ought to be the one for working and developing into a discourse. This might be done, but it would neither be expedient nor profitable. A passage at this moment offers itself to my eye—"Then said Isaiah to Hezekiah, Hear the word of the Lord of Hosts." This could be set up as the vehicle of instruction and persuasive earnestness; but it would not be sufficiently emphatic, as so many other verses bear a striking resemblance to it. Another passage now presents itself—"He causeth it to come, whether for correction, or for His land, or for mercy." An air of quaintness is about this verse, which makes it ineligible. Besides, the divisions are not homogeneous. Correction and mercy are related to each other. But if there be correction, it must be for some land; if there be a visitation of mercy, some favoured nation experiences it; so that the subject would, after all, include correction and mercy in their bearing and effects on any nation, and how a nation may become the meritorious object of either. But such a text would have great difficulties. Another portion, at the next opening of the Bible, presents itself (Joshua xxi. 26)— "All the cities were ten with their suburbs for the families of the children of Kohath that remained." This verse could hardly be made the subject of any exposition, except, perhaps, the Divine goodness displayed in the provision made from among the people for an ancient priesthood, or the benefit of a stated ministry. However, it is to be questioned if anyone would ever make such a verse a subject for the attention of an audience. Another passage from Numbers offers itself—"And they removed from Alush, and encamped at Rephidim, where was no water

for the people to drink." We know not how this could be made
the subject of the pulpit's exhibitions, unless it signified the
afflictions of the people of God in this life.

From the fact that it is not exactly as the Bible opens that
the preacher is to make selection of his text, is derived the
counterpart fact that he ought to be accurately acquainted with
the word of the Divine disclosures in all its parts, even those
most unfrequently perused. A mark might direct to particular
verses which contained subjects suitable or interesting. Thus
an ample store of text-material might be laid up. For instance,
on the uncertainty of life and employment of time, this verse
might be marked out—"Teach us to number our days, that we
may apply our hearts unto wisdom" (Psalm xc. 12). Or, for an
occasional sermon, this verse may have been noticed—"Train
up a child in the way he should go; and when he is old, he will
not depart from it" (Prov. xvii. 6). The following portion of
Scripture may serve as a text from which to explain and recommend the Gospel economy—"The Lord is well pleased for His
righteousness' sake : He will magnify the law, and make it
honourable" (Isaiah xlii. 21). The intrinsic excellency of that
morality which has taken the law of God for its basis, might be
unfolded and contrasted with other motives of action—such as
fashion, constitution, conveniency. "Little children, let no
man deceive you: he that doeth righteousness is righteous, even
as He is righteous." The difficulty here would be to treat the
subject without making it at all controversial, as the allusion
seems to be to a heresy which had arisen in the Church, which
attached nothing criminal to the worst actions, and no importance
to the most laudable performances, thus leading to conclude that
all actions were indifferent. The Apostle speaks of a modified
righteousness. He that doeth righteousness is, so far as his
actions of obedience go, righteous, and thus allied to the righteousness of God, so that He can look on such doings with
complacency, if they have been done on the principle of regard
to His will, and can receive them as evidences of an active
principle of obedience.

If it can be done, it is best to select a text which offers, in
itself, the line of thought which may only require amplification

and examples. For instance, in explaining the plan of Redemption, the following verse appears to present a fine opportunity for illustrating the Gospel truth, how all the severe prerogatives of Jehovah have been satisfied in the business of showing mercy to the sinner, so that by the atonement the most exacting attributes of the Godhead, instead of opposing the sinner on his path, are all now exercised in his favour—"Mercy and truth are met together: righteousness and peace have kissed each other" (Psalm lxxxv. 10).

A great deal of the difference between sermons may perhaps be ascribed to this Scriptural prefix to them. It cannot be expected that a text which only details some matter of history should be as productive of fine sentiment and ideas as one that contains the germ of these sentiments and ideas in itself. In the one, invention is required, and may not be successful. The other has only to be entered on; and it is supposed that where mind exists to be put into movement by great sentiments and sublimity of thought, the minister would have an easy task, since his work should be a work of mere enlargement; since he had to render more obviously patent that which was patent already; since the thoughts were outlined and seen in their embryo state, and had, when in that state, only to take hold of his intellect, to grow into a condition of obviousness and illustration.

It has to be confessed, after all, that preachers will be guided in their selection of texts, in a great measure, by their own studies, tastes, and mental peculiarities. And just as some natures delight in contemplating the alarming terrors of the Divine law, as Jonathan Edwards greatly loved to do, and may really think that to rend, alarm, and terrify with awful representations is the best preparation for the announcements which tell of the clemency of heaven's King, and His averted indignation, so others will enter on their work, and without any such formal notions regarding the necessity of an ordeal of pain, anguish or terror, will carry in their hands the cheering intelligence of a love that is never weary, and which cannot be turned out of its course by the ingratitude of man and all the hardened impenitence of rebellious nature. Some will thus delight to magnify and multiply the awful and brooding features of an incensed and wrathful law, and to produce the feeling of alarm and the tremors of those in evident jeopardy, and to move the soul out of the fastnesses of its delusions, and out of the power of those fallacies which bear it up in its delays and its neglect. These think that the representations which best bring to view and recollection Sinai, with all its fearful accompaniments— that "The voice of words," and the "Mountain burning with fire," and the breathing of that trumpet which "sounded long and loud," and caused the heart of the bravest Israelite to quail—are alone needful in stirring sinners to flee from the wrath which is before them, and take hold on eternal life. Another class are disposed to tender to the sinner, at his first setting out, the Son of God, "in whom is life eternal," and never discompose or terrify him with any alarming disclosures. The love of God for a sinful world is their grand idea of revelation.

But let us, to some extent, at least to the extent suited to the illustration of our subject, investigate the matter, and it will be found that diversities of constitution, taste or study, will have the effect in directing to those portions of Scripture really beneficial, as there will be in an assembled society the same difference of constitution and preference. The tendencies of him who occupies the pulpit will represent those of at least a large number of his hearers. The people will thus be enabled to sympathise sufficiently where there is a strong mental bias in any one direction. Whether it be on what is affecting in the Divine government that the minister delights to expatiate, he will be sure of a large portion who will acquiesce in those descriptions which alarm. He will thus be in the way of becoming a useful preacher to that congregation, modified by this circumstance—that, in the opinion of others, there will be a drawback in his ministrations, because he does not give that prominence to the love of God which they think he should. But they will soon come to be more generally pleased with his mode of instruction. But should the favourite topic be "the love of God, which passeth knowledge," and he be averse from those awful and terrifying descriptions, then the class inclined to think that the way to Calvary is past the voices, flames, and thunderings of Sinai, will at first be disposed to blame him for a theology so mild and condescending in its offers. After some time, however, the general sentiment will be that under his ministry their souls are prospering, and disciples multiplying.

There will thus be an increasing regard for those views which are most frequently brought before their notice, and for those texts which serve as the channel of their exemplification.

But let it be ever remembered that Christ was a model, as well as a reconciling and sweet-smelling sacrifice, and that He has left His disciples an ensample that they should follow in His steps. And the Scriptures are by no means lacking in those exhortations and statements which may serve as the groundwork on which to build up the disciple of Christ, adorned with every virtue fitted to obtain the approval of humanity, as well as with the knowledge which tells of the wonders of Redemption. The object of the Christian advocate is surely to bring out to clear manifestation, on the person of the believer, all the virtues which are thought to enter into a Christian character. Whether it be the loveliness of charity, the rigour of justice, the self-denying virtue of temperance, the resignation of patience, the grandeur of forbearance, the self-sustaining power and endurance of principle, let the genuine ambassador of Christ betake himself to his grand text-book, and he will surely find in its pages as much as will enable him to add living disciples to the faith. It only requires the faith of the Christian minister to do so. This faith will take him frequently to the great Teacher. At His feet he will learn wisdom. The words of His lips will be regarded as more precious than the gold of Ophir, "sweeter also than honey and the honeycomb."

CHAPTER V.

THE COMPOSITION OF A SERMON.

"The preacher sought to find out acceptable words" (Eccles. xii. 10).

THE next subject which now comes to be considered is the composition of sermons, which is nothing more nor less than arranging a number of words and sentences, on any particular subject, so as to produce the effect intended. This may be to move, to instruct, or to improve. Indeed, for conveying our conceptions or impressions to the mind of others, so as to make them feel and be affected as we are ourselves, it is necessary to have recourse to language; that is, to some arrangement of words; that is, to composition. Words are, in this arrangement, signs of ideas; and it is not by the conveyance of the ideas themselves that we make ourselves intelligible to the mind of others, but by the medium of words so arranged and selected that they may produce the thought in the mind of others with the clearness with which we perceive it ourselves.

Thus, an unpremeditated or extemporaneous sally of the mind, whatever the subject may be, is composition. It is an instinctive collocation of words, arranged as best to affect others. Whatever strongly moves our passions, elicits our gratitude, or impresses by a feeling of awe or danger, impels us to an effort of composition which is, at the same time, grateful to our natures, as it may be the means of making others participate in our gladness, or of abating the anguish of some disagreeable emotion or painful sensation. It might, therefore, be received as an axiom, that composition will attain its greatest excellence when the sentiments are lively and the conceptions clear.

The difference between written and oral composition is only in the circumstances in which the writer and mere speaker are placed. Composition on paper is distinguished from extemporaneous effort by many circumstances which tend to give the former a superiority over the latter. One of these circumstances is the unhurried state of the mind turned to the subject or general topic, on which it is to bring forth its treasures, whether of previous thought or previous information which it had collected. This can hardly be done where the mind, from beginning to end, is not allowed to take any rest, so as to consider what part of a subject is best for some specific design. The student, therefore, who sits down to the transference of his own meditations to paper, is likely to be rewarded by a creation of the mind far grander and far more precious than anything which would have resulted from an effort in connection with a subject which had really never undergone the *acies* of his intellect, and from the thorough examination of which he, by the circumstances, was prevented.

In his leisure moments, the power of thought or contemplation will grow into an effervescence which will render his composition far more effective than when pressed and hurried forward with a speed which rushes before the effort of his reflection to keep pace with it. He must then, of consequence, utter much which is childish and insipid, and which offends against the proprieties of good taste and arrangements of correct language. If the mind be of that character that it finds something new, the verbal expression given to it will be greatly inadequate to the production of an impression on others. If the mind is not of this character, the efforts will be always tending to some familiar track of amplification to which they have been used and cannot easily avoid. The sentiments will be uttered without examination; and, in the declamatory temerity of the moment, a great deal, unless the mind be of a particular class, will escape, which in leisure moments will receive condemnation.

When the mind is exerting its whole power of contemplation in private, it is probable that a subject will expand itself, under such an exercise of the mental powers, into those sentences, paragraphs, and generalities which will render it most effective. Just as the man who takes his aerial post on some eminence has, from that speculative elevation, a prospect which he may divide into all its topical distinctions of valley or rising ground, city or hamlet, river or forest. As he extends his view, more of the features of the landscape emerge out of remoteness and concealment; while he who hurries with the precipitancy and despatch of modern travelling is deprived of the opportunity of observation by the speed at which he is carried. There is the same difference between the expenditure of pains and time, and the rapid and ofttimes careless preparations of the extemporaneous orator. In the leisure of the closet, it is almost impossible but that new forms and combinations of language and conception will offer themselves.

Another important distinction, which gives a superiority to the composition of the closet, is that in the privacy of the study recourse can be had to some standards by which to become more particularly acquainted with the point you intend to discuss. There are collected, around the meditative occupant, those silent monitors, ready to extend their advice and information, without giving the offence which more noisy monitors can hardly avoid. Certain authorities are ranged around, and when a difficulty occurs, or the proper incentive is wanting, or a hitherto unthought-of sentiment enters the mind, these may be resorted to for the purpose of settling the difficulty, bringing the thoughts into the tone necessary for the proper and spirited treatment of the subject, or giving weight to the sentiment you have entertained or intend to set forth.

It is related of the celebrated French preacher Bossuet, whose pulpit exhibitions were generally extemporaneous efforts, but efforts of a mind furnished with an immense copiousness of matter, and always at a white heat with some great emotion, that previous to his entering the pulpit he had recourse for the requisite excitement to a chapter of Isaiah or a page of Homer. It is strange that they are classed together; but we suppose it was on the principle that whatever was the stimulant for the occasion, it was morally right to accept it for the sake of the effect. If this exercise was of any importance in those efforts where the language is unprepared, it might be needful, even when the ordeal must be passed, of expanding before the eye opinions, thoughts, and sentiments. To create fervour or give dignity, it may be of importance to make the effort to expand the soul beneath the fervour or ideas of an external auxiliary.

Books will be found a great source of power, not so much by imparting information, as exciting the dormant or languishing faculties, and getting them into that state of fervency required for the most successful attempts at composition. By them the mind is moved out of its apathy. The collision of thought with thought is found to be useful in giving rise to those beauteous creations of feeling or fancy which will end in profit and delight. The art of composition will be attained most readily, and reach its highest degree of cultivation, in the preacher who has devoted much of his time to the finest specimens of its excellencies.

But written excels spoken composition from the fact that the mind becomes habituated to those quiet and silent trains of thought which are needful when a subject is to be transferred, in all the ceremony of letters, words, and paragraphs, to the paper before us. The mind knows what it has to do, and, when put to the task, finds no great difficulty in gathering its various resources together, and collecting from all quarters whatever is demanded for the discharge of its duties. Whatever style of composition it is used to becomes easier the more the intellect is habituated to it. Its powers grow by use and are enlarged by action. Whatever is demanded from it, the demand will be met if the power has been used to it. You cannot invite its exercise in vain if it is a wonted exercise.

The power or facility certainly grows with the amount of composition produced. It is astonishing what an immense mass of it may accumulate in a few years. Perhaps it is the apprehension of this abundance which deters from this delightful exercise. People think when they have produced so much they may relax their exertions and produce no more. They need not, therefore, wonder that their style diminishes in power, that their materials decrease in quantity and value, that their words are badly selected, and their whole an "indigesta moles."

In a mind at all favoured with sensibilities, words will so put themselves together as to produce a natural harmony and cadence. This will be rendered obvious from the following quotation, taken from *Hanna's Life of Dr. Chalmers*, describing the heaviness of the family's bereavement when they were compelled, on the death of the minister, to exchange the quiet rural manse for the strangeness of a world so little familiar to them:—" When the sons and daughters of clergymen are left to go, they know not whither, from the peacefulness of their father's dwelling, never were poor outcasts less prepared, by the education and the habits of former years, for the scowl of an unpitying world; nor can I figure a drearier and more affecting contrast than that which obtains between the blissful security of their earlier days and the dark and unshielded condition to which the hand of Providence has now brought them. It is not necessary, for the purpose of awakening your sensibilities on this subject, to dwell on every one circumstance of distress which enters into the sufferings of this bereaved family; or to tell you of the many friends they must abandon, and the many charms of that peaceful neighbourhood which they must quit for ever. But when they look abroad and survey the innumerable beauties which the God of nature has scattered so profusely around them; when they see the sun throwing its unclouded splendours over the whole neighbourhood; when, on the fair side of the year, they behold the smiling aspect of the country, and, at every footstep they take, some flower appears in its loveliness, or some bird offers its melody to delight them; when they see quietness on all the hills, and every field glowing in the pride and luxury of vegetation; when they see summer throwing its rich garment over this goodly scene of magnificence and glory, and think, in the bitterness of their souls, that this is the last summer which they shall ever witness smiling on that scene, which all the ties of habit and of affection have endeared to them; when this thought, melancholy as it is, is lost and overborne in the far darker melancholy of a father torn from their embrace, and a helpless family left to find their way, unprotected and alone, through the lowering futurity of this earthly pilgrimage, Do you wonder that their feeling hearts should be ready to lose hold of the promise, that 'He who decks the lily fair in flowery pride' will guide them in safety through the world, and, at last, raise all who believe on Him to the bloom and the vigour of immortality? 'The flowers of the field they toil not, neither do they spin; yet your Heavenly Father careth for them; and how much more careth He for you, O ye of little faith.'" We are informed that the audience was as much moved by this affecting passage as the speaker, and that it was a swell of unparalleled eloquence.

We now give another specimen from the sermons of this great preacher. Making an effort to demolish that dependence which men are inclined to place on a death-bed repentance, this great man thus says:—"And what, what, we would ask, is the scene in which you are now purposing to contest it with all this mighty force of opposition you are now so busy in raising up against you? What is the field of combat to which you are now looking forward as the place where you are to accomplish a victory over all those formidable enemies whom you are at present arming with such a weight of hostility, as we say, within a single hair-breadth of certainty, you will find to be irresistible? Oh, the folly of such a misleading infatuation! The proposed scene on which this battle for eternity is to be fought, and this victory for the crown of glory is to be won, is a death-bed. It is when the last messenger stands by the couch of the dying man, and shakes at him the terrors of his grisly countenance, that the poor child of infatuation thinks he is to struggle and prevail against all his enemies; against the unrelenting tyranny of habit; against the obstinacy of his own heart, which he is now doing so much to harden; against the Spirit of God who perhaps long ere now has pronounced the doom upon him—'He will take his own way, and walk in his own counsel; I shall cease from striving and let him alone'; against Satan, to whom, every day of his life, he has given some fresh advantage over him, and who will not be willing to lose the victim, on whom he has practised so many wiles, and plied with success so many delusions. And such are the enemies whom you, who wretchedly calculate on the repentance of the eleventh hour, are every day mustering up in greater force and formidableness against you; and how can we think of letting you go with any other repentance than the repentance of the precious moment that is now passing over you, when we look forward to the horrors of that impressive scene on which you propose to win the prize of immortality, and to contest it, single-handed and alone, with all the weight of opposition which you have accumulated against yourselves—a death-bed—a languid, tossing, breathless, and agitated death-bed; that scene of feebleness, where the poor man cannot help himself to a single mouthful; when he must have attendants to sit around him and watch his every wish, and interpret his every signal, and turn him to every posture, where he may find a moment's ease, and wipe away the cold sweat that is running over him, and ply him with cordials for thirst, and sickness, and insufferable languor! And this is the time, when occupied with such feelings, and beset with such agonies as these, you propose to crowd, within the compass of a few wretched days, the work of winding up the concerns of a neglected eternity." He who witnessed the delivery of this astonishing description has told us, that under it the audience were swayed to and fro, as a forest swept by a hurricane.

This class of composition might be spoken of as the amplified and gorgeous. Circumstance follows on circumstance. It looks as if the author tried to what extent he might enlarge or expand a particular event; in one case, a minister's family, on their father's death, leaving the residence provided for him; in the other, an impenitent sinner on his dying bed, struggling with those inexorable foes to whom delay and neglect have imparted such power. Though the paragraphs, it is likely, were produced at one effort, and were then as good as could be, yet the finest polish which diction receives from art could not compare with that natural cadence and harmony they are found to possess. It shows what verbiage and amplification can do when sustained by a strong internal sentiment. It will be seen that they are as different from the bombastic platitudes of the writer who, without the fervour and fire of their author, should attempt this kind of style, as the effort of the man compelled to some deed of daring or strength, by the strong sense of danger or by fear, is different from his performance when trying the same act in the indolence of repose or for mere amusement. Such a style of composition may be possessed naturally, but can never be imitated with any degree of success. To produce it requires an idiosyncrasy. It is the result of original fervour and native susceptibilities. And as the imitation of it cannot produce these internal emotions from which it springs, so all the effort expended would be lost, without fervour in the writing, and such agonizing energy in the delivery as nature seldom imparts.

We could, by no means, therefore, recommend imitation,

unless the style has in it something like that for which by nature we are adapted. Without a native fire of glowing and generous impulse, without a genuine taste for what is sublime and beautiful in nature, without great and original faculties of observation, all effort would be in vain. It is not a style to be acquired; for it is the picture of an internal nature which can never be acquired. It is not a style which art or diligence can confer; for, in one sense, it is not artificial, as it is more a process of the intellect exhibited before the eye. *The Spectator*, *The Rambler*, may be models; and, because they are generally tame and uniform, may be imitated; but the majesty of this master of eloquence cannot be borrowed, because it is the mark of an internal nature which cannot be imparted.

The best productions of the human mind, and the finest models which present the excellencies of composition, are always marked by two great characteristics—intensity of feeling and vividness of conception. That magical arrangement of words and sentences, which has such power, is mainly derived from intensity and clearness. This does not mean profoundness of thought or philosophic clearness. The profoundest thinkers are not, sometimes, possessed of these qualities, as Locke, Butler, Reid, or even Mills in our own day. This vividness belongs to external nature, and is pictured on the observant mind, and reflected back again on other minds. Those who excel in brightness of conception possess this quality in its perfection, when something which was before the object of the senses becomes, as it were, the object of some internal vision. And this peculiar kind of composition cannot but be delightful, because thought or impressions are conveyed by the employment of images or illustrations which are every day the objects of visions.

Intensity is perhaps distinct from vividness of conceiving, in this respect—that intensity contains somewhat of the emotional, clearness somewhat of the intellectual. Intensity carries with it the notion of the painful or oppressive, vividness of light and brightness. A conception is intense when we labour under it, or wish to convey the full impression of it into the mind of another. It is vivid when it is sparkling. If once seen, a person may have a clear conception of meandering rills, meadows embroidered with flowers and carpeted with verdure, or intermingled woods, or lawns, or palaces. All is here delightful. No violent emotion is excited. But intensity of conception gives an idea of something painfully vivid, which carries an emotion with it. A person with intensity of conception is pursued by his mental delineations. They will not let him rest. But on pictures too vivid, he has the power of resolutely putting a quietus, by diverting his attention from them and fixing it on something else.

But let no one think to attain excellency in composition without copiousness of matter. Where the mind is such that it loves meditation, or readily assimilates, enlarges and improves the reflection of other minds, there will be a supply of material which cannot be expended. With a mind like this, a suggestion becomes the first link in a chain of ever-increasing links, of which chain it would seem as if one link were, by some strange law of mind, the efficient cause of its successor. But for the general mind, which is rather an acquirer than inventor, copiousness of matter will only be acquired by reading; and that reading ought to be of the best books. Some thoughts, embodied by meditation, will give rise to a style of composition which the *dicta* of mere prescription could never produce. Indeed, it need not be wondered that the man who will never give himself to the toils of actual meditation, or the effort to incorporate with his own, the ideas and meditations of other minds,—whose idea of the ministerial function is that it consists in effecting something which can be done by hands or feet,— that it is a profession in which, without any interval for real thought, one laborious and visible performance hurries on another, and that thus, before the world's eye, the appearance is kept up of incessant activity,—that this man will not be able to attain to any advancement in the art of polished composition, though making up for it by discharge of important duty.

There are many and widely-varying kinds of composition which will commend themselves to minds suited to them. There is the picturesque kind, in which every word is a picture, and figures are presented in a succession of words. There is that

E

which is condensed and solid, without a redundancy or expletive. The admirers of this style direct us to obliterate every word not absolutely required—a very effectual method for abbreviating and curtailing most productions. Others, however, enjoin us to amplify and enlarge, and that time and experience will reduce verbosity to a graceful and becoming conciseness. These two distinct advices proceed from the highest authorities. In such circumstances, it is not easy to know what precise plan to adopt— whether to prune luxuriencies or allow time to give experience.

Epithets and enumerations may, however, have their own use, and by lopping away what was rich and gorgeous we may, instead of improving, be really destroying—just as in a painting, to efface a particular line may be the destruction of a necessary feature. To say simply "God is good," is stating His character as concisely as it can be given; but to say that "He gives rain from heaven and fruitful seasons, filling our hearts with food and gladness," is expanding the attribute of goodness into its particulars. Some could not bear to call life a "pilgrimage," much less to speak of it as "a laborious and painful pilgrimage, whose gloomy path was strowed with thorns, obstructed by perpetual obstacles, and mantled with the clouds of misery and despair." But however this may be opposed to the idea of conciseness, it is the way of stating a fact most forcibly to those who have a mind to reflect and a heart to be affected.

The order of composition adapted to the expositions of the clergyman is, without any doubt, that which is diffusive, rather than concise. There is a difference, however, between this expansiveness and the platitudes which the ill-prepared speaker has to utter. A subject may be expanded with elegance and ability, and is rather a gainer by the enlargement. Platitude takes place where there is a painful abundance of words, with an evident absence of matter and thought. The person who utters a platitude is like the person who utters a truism. Platitude expands the same amount of air into a larger space by taking from its density. Expansion makes more space for a larger amount of air. There is no intellectual delight in plati- tude. There is an intellectual pleasure in expansion. Platitude repeats and re-repeats without any more variety than another

set of vocables. Expansion takes in more territory. For every
addition there is a change of scene. To be chargeable with
making platitudes is to be accused of want of intellect. Expansiveness is a sign of the most exuberant intellect.

Composition fitted to set forth the claims of religion, and
therefore fitted to the genius of the pulpit, admits of that which
other compositions rarely do. It is even adorned and finished
by exclamation. However, exclamation must be employed with
rarity. "But what are the hopes of man," says Johnson on a
mournful occasion; "I am disappointed by that stroke of death,
which has eclipsed the gaiety of nations, and impoverished
the public stock of harmless pleasure!" The minister of
Kilmaney employs the following exclamatory clause on the death
of the Princess Charlotte—"O death, thou hast indeed chosen
the time and the victim for demonstrating the grim ascendancy
of thy power over all the hopes and fortunes of our species!"
On the death of Crassus, Cicero makes almost the same lament,
and speaks about the death of Crassus in a manner worthy of
the applause of a Christian—"ut mihi non erepta L. Crasso, à
diis immortalibus vita, sed donata mors esse videatur." His
death is thus lamented—"O fallacem hominum spem, fragil-
emque fortunam, et inanes nostras contentiones, quae in medio
spatio saepe franguntur et corruunt, et, ante in ipso cursu,
obruunter, quam portum conspicere potuerunt."

We may now describe the methods by which the great
Roman master of philosophy and eloquence declares himself to
have arrived at such excellency. The remark of Cicero is well
known, that the orator is akin to the poet, inasmuch as the one
is almost as rarely met with as the other; that both have
faculties which occupy a common territory, though the one in
some respects commands a region which the other does not.
Great susceptibility, brilliant fancy, and strong imagination, are
common to each. Each traverses a general territory, and yet
has a province, the length and breadth of which is not traversed
by the other.

In his "De Oratore," Cicero delivers a judgment at once
true and profound, that "the pen is the most powerful cause
and the great teacher of eloquence." It is truly a judicious

decision. The man who holds the labour of the scribe in contempt; who is moved by a strong dislike of paper; who boasts that he is superior to the necessity of expanding his thoughts on paper, has probably not many thoughts to expand, and can only be distinguished by an empty fluency and grotesque gestures. The learned Roman most explicitly declares that all the topics and salient points worth our attention, as we are writing and contemplating the subject with the power of intellect, spontaneously offer themselves, and all the words and sentences which we require arrange themselves under the point of the pen; not only that, but arrange themselves like skilfully ordered soldiers, "quodam oratorio numero et modo," with a certain cadence and measure.

Another exercise this illustrious consul tells us he indulged in was, the reading of large portions from the Greek writers, and then declaiming the same in Latin, as eloquently as he could for words and sentences. In another place he tells us it was his habit to suppose subjects, and questions, and clients, whose cause he had to plead, and on these imaginary cases he used the most select and dignified words and sentiments he could select. With a strong natural tendency to express his thoughts in the purest language, he at last attained the palm of eloquence, so that no contemporary, neither Crassus nor the courtly Hortensius, could compete with him. His works are the most voluminous, intelligible, and best preserved which have remained from ancient times.

In concluding this division of our subject, let us advert to the ideas which seem to be in the ascendant regarding the composition of sermons. Let us examine them, and discover, if we can, to what extent they bear the application of certain laws which have a currency on the matter of general composition as it is fitted to reach and affect the human mind. And, first, it is affirmed that nothing can, by any possibility, do good unless what is very simply expressed, and the high authority by which this opinion is to find its vindication, is affirmed to be the Author of Christianity Himself. It is asserted that He employed, in His parables and addresses to the multitude, the simplest and most unadorned language. The grandeur of human eloquence was

lost in it. The figures of a terrestrial rhetoric found no place
.there.

It might be asked, then, was this a simplicity in mere
sentiments or in words? His speech was, no doubt, very pure;
and yet where feeling was necessary, and where fervour gave rise
to expansion, the language of Christ was by no means devoid of
what is deemed the antipodes of simplicity. It is true a verse
here and there may be discovered where purity of language has
reached its climax. "Behold the fowls of the air, they sow not,
neither do they reap, nor gather into barns; yet your Heavenly
Father feedeth them." This is, in one sense, by no means
simple. The advocacy of a Divine Providence from the fowls
being supplied with food is simple; but the contrasting of them
with sowers and reapers is not. But Christ's language in the
twenty-third of Matthew, that chapter of weighty denunciation
against scribes and Pharisees, is not a sample, by any means,
of the style of the *purist* in language. Its language is select
without being too much so, and circumstances are added to one
another almost to tediousness. The language of the Apostle of
the Gentiles is exceedingly grand, and his style complicated.
The ardour of his mind carried him away into a subject or
circumstance which had little or no connection with his main
design. He is replete with parenthetical clauses, even to
obscurity. He appears to have given free vent to his fervour,
and where it led him to enumeration, or exclamation, or enlargement, he was not very attentive to that exceeding clarity
of style so highly recommended.

Those who maintain the cause of the simplest style, do not
always intend by that any clearness more than belongs to other
modes of writing. By that are meant, in their opinion, sentences
never exceeding a line in length, and words seldom more than
one syllable. They would object to such expressions as "demonstration of the Spirit," and "after ye were illuminated," and
sundry others from inspiration. If a body of people consisted
of members ranging rather below the average of human intellect,
they might make a plea for a notion which seems to be a misconception of the whole matter. But composed, as congregations
are, of some of the finest intellects, we hope that no one,

naturally endowed with a taste for the elegant in language or the comprehensive in thought, will stunt his native tendencies down to the taste of the admirers of what is so exceedingly simple.

The great consideration which all this leads to is, that each one will do best by finding that class of composition to which his disposition and tendencies adapt him, and by giving it almost full scope. Of Thomson, we are informed, in the. Life of the Author of the "Seasons," by Dr. Johnson, that being called on by his teacher of Theology to deliver a probationary exercise, by an explanation of a Psalm, "his diction was so poetically splendid, that Mr. Hamilton, the professor of Divinity, reproved him for speaking language unintelligible to a popular audience." After all, were that essay of the young poet-student to be discovered, it might perhaps be found that his language was not so much out of the range of ordinary humanity, and that, in general, audiences are not so ignorant as not to know what a youth might inform them of, and know it by the language he employed.

It is just possible that many a high-thinking youth has been repressed in his ardour by those who employ rules instead of ability, and who are distinguished by a few frigid maxims instead of that penetration by which they might discover the qualities within. Rules are not intended to usurp the place of nature, but to limit her vagaries and regulate her flame. They derive their importance from nature, but cannot convey mind where it is defective, and are not intended to repress it where it appears.

It is the minister's duty, instead of thinking that his tastes and talents are too high, and consequently bringing them down to a lower level, to try and raise that level higher in the scale both of principle and information. By the well-informed of the community, no compact is understood by which the ambassador of Christ is to lower the standard either of taste or principle. It would, indeed, be a sad and woeful desecration. Those who know the people do not believe there is any such demand on their part. Rising themselves higher every day on the scale of knowledge, they are prepared for as learned a ministry as can be given them. Nor will ardour of intellect or feats of scholarship be any obstacle in the way of appreciating such a ministry.

CHAPTER VI.

THE PREPARATION OF A SERMON FOR DELIVERY.

ALL the exercises of the closet, and processes of thought which are there performed, have one general object, direct or indirect, namely, that preparation whereby the whole man, "body, soul, and spirit," is put in a state to make a proper impression and praiseworthy exhibition in the pulpit. By praiseworthy, it is not meant to lower the high functions of the ministry of the Word to a vain and paltry eye-service, to catch that applause which cometh from man, and to lose the praise which is of God. It is because of the excellency and honour which, we think, belong to this office; it is because we would wish all which concerns it to be done decently, or at least not give to any, other offence than what is essentially connected with its high position as being a rebuke, "a rock of offence" to the unchristian world; as being the seat from which the sinner is reproached with his ingratitude, and arrested, if possible, in his infatuation, and brought back unto the Being from whom he has so signally departed.

These considerations, connected with ministerial duty, are no doubt fitted to solemnize and make one enquire, Who is sufficient for a work so sacred and awful? When Moses was asked to assume the functions of leader and chief, he exclaims, looking at his unworthiness, "O my Lord, I am not eloquent, neither heretofore, nor since Thou hast spoken unto Thy servant; but I am slow of speech, and of a slow tongue." He deprecates being called to undertake such responsibility. He says, I will not undertake a task so onerous. And surely if any argument is of power to cause the teacher of Christianity to do it, as "a workman that needs not to be ashamed," it is the feeling that, for the proper discharge of his mission, he will be held accountable; and that, if there be labour or effort by which his preparations could have been rendered more effectual in delivering souls from the bonds of iniquity, and bringing them into the region of Gospel light and enlargement, and if he have not undergone this

attempt the hasty exposition is, in the young minister, unless of very fine abilities, or indeed formed for it, an act of great temerity, and is wanting in sufficient homage to that Word which professes to come from the Father of Enlightenment.

It is said to be "the glory of God to conceal a thing." If He has hidden in obscurity the mysteries of His economy, it is to put the human mind on the stretch to unfold and bring forth to the light these, not "the hidden things of darkness," but things veiled with a mantle of obscurity, until labour and study draw aside that curtain, and manifest them in their glory and effulgence. Those occasional seasons are not meant in which the circumstances demand the words of an unprepared and not altogether studied eloquence. But that any should make a habitual practice of delaying preparation till no time for it is left, seems irreconcilable with a due discharge of a great and important function.

Indeed, we know not if there be any such thing as to speak strictly and literally *extempore*. The previous meditations may not have been those of a moment previous, but a day, or week, or a month. The mind may certainly and involuntarily return to a process of thought which, in the excitement of the moment, it may perform again. But to expatiate on a topic which has never, in any way, been the object of the mind's inspection, and to which the attention has at no time been directed, seems irreconcilable with the nature of the mind. We know not what kind of exuberance that would be which could exact from the mind thoughts duly regulated, and expressions properly correct, on a subject to which the attention was never directed. It seems indispensable that, at some time, a subject should have been the topic of the mind's contemplation to speak of it at all.

Another style of preparation for the pulpit is from notes which have been previously written with more or less care. This, we apprehend, as it is done with facility, is done pretty generally, and, perhaps, if done with taste and fulness, would be a practice sufficiently suitable. We are afraid, however, it may not be always proper, but may lead to hurried and uncommented views of a subject, and to those divisions and infinite sub-divisions which figure so much in "Skeletons of

Sermons," which would lead one to suppose that a sermon ought
to possess an exhaustive effect on any particular subject, and
ramify in all directions. It would look like giving such a
number of chances, that success would be the natural result.
If it was not so easy to dilate on one particular proposition,
another may visit the mind with more suggestiveness. Hastily
quitting one division, the next may be more familiar.

Speaking in this way has one advantage, that it is not
necessary to adhere so closely to the scheme of the discourse,
but that, according to time, place, and circumstance, the person
may deviate and enlarge, and even invent as he proceeds. New
ideas may offer in a way which will make them acceptable, and
show the propriety of attending to them. The mind, in pursuit
of its premeditated ideas, may fall in with fortuitous ones more
edifying and instructive. In the warmth and transport of the
moment, the soul may break through the chilling fetters of
ceremony into a new and before unthought-of region, rich in
many of the objects of thought, and rewarding it for the irrup-
tion it has made into an unfamiliar but congenial territory.
The power of novelty may give an impulse it never before had
experienced.

Thus, if this text were taken from the last chapter of the
book of Job—" I have heard of Thee by the hearing of the ear; but
now mine eye seeth Thee: wherefore I abhor myself, and repent in
dust and ashes," the general division is obvious, and three particulars are included in the verses. First, it would naturally be
enquired what the hearing of Him by the ear did signify, and
when we did thus hear of God. In connection with this division,
it might be said that the light reflected from His works was
actually the same as hearing of Him by the hearing of the ear;
their reports of God were so ambiguous, the light so feeble and
insufficient. Hearing of a person is, by no means, the same as
seeing him. His works convey faint whispers of Him, but never
reveal the unsearchable Maker in the grandeur of His attributes,
or mysteriousness of His essence. Philosophy, science, art,
history, may give forth some intimations, but cannot reveal Him
in His love or condescension.

The enquiry would arise, in the second part, What was

meant by the view of God? He had answered Job out of the whirlwind, and effused on his understanding such a knowledge of His ways, and experience of His mysterious presence throughout the vast limits of His immense sovereignty, and such a concern in the afflictions of the patriarch, and vindication of him from the unkind aspersions of his friends, that it was like a view of God, in which was rendered obvious his own insignificance. What he had heard did not affect him. It was the near view of God which he had obtained that sunk him into dust and ashes; which means, that he obtained such a view of God's mysterious wisdom in His providential dealings, that he beheld his utter incompetency to pronounce the sentence on his Maker. He beheld the evidence of a wisdom and righteousness far above his own. He was humbled for his amazing and excessive presumption in attempting to pronounce what God should do with His offspring that had strayed away. He saw his own unholiness, and beheld the transparent purity of Him in whose sight "the heavens are unclean, and whose angels are charged with folly." A new light was reflected from the view of God Himself, as distinct from all we can learn from His works, on the soul of the prophet. In that light he beheld his vileness, and the dust and ashes were the symbols of his humility.

Natural excitement might give rise to new ideas in connection with God; and the reports, emptied into the ear, might be shown to be wholly different from some awful manifestation which He may make of Himself, as in the sweeping devastations of the tempest, in the blinding glare of the lightning, in the awful reverberations of the thunder, or in the movement of the human heart, agonized from a sense of its sins, and agitated by the question, "How shall I appear before God"? If He could thus appear in open visibility, it would, no doubt, be amid such movements of His works as would be fitted to convulse and to alarm.

The view of a God so transcendent in holiness, would show Him equally transcendent in wisdom, and naturally cause the patriarch to repent of the readiness with which he ventured to pronounce on doings which have their work and consummation in eternity. This would also be the effect of the declaration of

God's law. The seeing of God by the eye might also refer to that experimental view of the love of God or His justice, so fitted to fill the heart with direful forebodings, or hopeful confidence.

There is, again, a species of eloquence or delivery which may be said to be extemporaneous, from the fact that it is the impression which a sermon written, but not committed to the storehouse of memory, by the severe labour of conning sentence after sentence, has left on the mind. In this case it is not expected that words can be recalled. Thus new ideas may intervene; as, in the emotion of the moment, the memory may recall but a small portion of the discourse. Yet, if the preacher have a taste for this exercise, and power in the delivery of ideas which the mind has been employed in committing to paper after their discovery, it is, perhaps, the surest way of bestowing a fluency at once ready, ardent, and correct.

The practice of previous writing is supposed not only to strengthen the mind in its power to retain ideas on the field of thought, but to create, invent, and arrange. Thoughts take their natural order when expanded before the eye. And though the individual were to allow what is written to go into as utter oblivion as if it had not been written, yet good is the result. The powers of mind are aroused to their greatest exercise, and it is most likely that the writer, when used to the task of writing, will be able to think more accurately and profitably, and invest his thoughts in more becoming garb, than if, simply without any attempt at composition, he reviewed the matter on the surface, discovered its salient points, and, with few and inadequate ideas, ventured on the irksome task of doling out his unfinished sentences and crude conceptions.

And thus, if every sermon had actually been written, even though not a sentence of it were engraven on the tablet of memory, by the effort of committing, it is not to be supposed that such an effort at writing could be sustained without a positive and beneficial result, perceptible in the clearness of thought and finish of composition. And if it be true, that *without labour nature has given nothing to mortals*, it must be equally true that when there has been an outlay of effort and energy, it will be rendered manifest in the superiority of the article produced. A principle largely dwelt upon, and developed in the written composition, will more equably expand itself before the speaker's mind. This mode will not be found at all to diminish promptness and energy. The man will be readier who has written largely, and who on paper has called on his mental resources, than he who has never written, or only in producing notes which indicate the leading and prominent particulars to be expanded.

Facility of writing grows according to frequency; and it is most likely that facility of extemporaneous utterance will be vastly promoted by the amount of written composition which has been produced. The man who after having travelled over the contents of several pages can give not the words, but facts and sentiments of these pages, expressed in his own language, is, perhaps, much superior in real intellect to the person whose adhesive and tenacious memory has taken the impression of the words without being cognizant, at the same time, of the ideas contained in them. To gather a just impression from the intellectual element of a treatise is, it may be, a higher reach of intellect than to acquire the words in which the ideas are embodied. Mere words are like those deposits in a pipe or conduit which may at last obstruct the passage of the fluid. To have a mind which can thus become a receptacle for mere verbiage is to have a very useful, but not perhaps an originating, class of intellect. A mind of this description will not be disturbed by any effervescence or by great inventiveness. No great sublimities of thought will acclerate a rapid approach to that paper which is to receive them; but it is better to be useful than sublime.

Writing has this advantage, that it provides a sufficient vocabulary without detracting from the pleasure which exists in discovering and following out new ideas. It gives words without making each word a painful idea. It gives them as the rudimental parts of a sentence; and we know that sentence in Latin expressed the notion of an arrangement of words, and the sentiment contained in them. A sentence should thus, at least, represent a sentiment, contain a thought, and not be a mere arrangement of words "signifying nothing." It might consist of many or few words. To utter it might take more or less time. We know not that there is any settled rule on the matter; but its effectiveness will always arise from the amount of mind contained in it. It will be likely, also, that the speaker who is used to the formation of sentences on paper, will be best able to produce them on the spot when occasion demands.

All critics will attest it as a most important truth in mental science, that labour bestowed on the artificial structure of sentences is not in vain. Art, in some shape or form, must belong to all writing intended to have the effect of impressing and affecting. And if nature has so favoured any of her sons that his diction and style seem to be possessed more than acquired, to have effect he must deceive those who know not the exuberant fountain from which they have emanated, by presenting the appearance of painful attention and labour. A few minds may be so gifted and favoured that their unpremeditated efforts take the form of highest art and elegance. Like a mighty, impetuous, and fertilizing stream, its plains abounding in luxuriant harvests, and its banks adorned with flowers, so there may be a natural facility of description and excogitation—the outflow of a mind incandescent with conceptions, and, like a magician, producing dazzling brilliancies and beauties of thought and expression at the same moment; its feelings so lively, and sensibilities so fine, that glowing and beauteous shapes belong to its very essence. These will naturally clothe themselves in the best language; and yet when the being thus gifted betakes himself to the toils of the composer, his vigorous and ready eloquence is as much surpassed by his written and laboured preparations as the former might be said to excel the extemporaneous effort of him whose mind is not so lively nor matter so abundant.

We have before ventured the opinion, that the best sermons were written. Should any one seem to extemporize sermons which present a high degree of excellency, they may owe it to a former habit of writing, now no longer necessary. Of the celebrated Robert Hall, it is said that he was accustomed to prepare and put together long paragraphs of solid and well-wrought composition, and confine them in his thoughts till they were required. It was, however, a practice for which, it is said, he suffered severely afterwards—a practice, probably, opposed to the nature of the human faculties, and by no means to be recommended. As far as the nature of the intellect can be ascertained, it seems to be this: it receives a suggestion; sees that it may be interesting or important; finds that it admits of expansion; proceeds to commit it, with the accessories of diction and illustration, to paper. The conclusion is obvious that beyond this no one should, by any consideration, be tempted to go.

But are these the only prescribed and legitimate methods of preparation? Do these meet the demands, exigencies, and peculiar qualities of every intellect? Provided all these rules be observed, is there no fear of any intellect going to loss because it cannot, without lowering its faculties and diminishing its usefulness, act in compliance with them? The best orations of Cicero, as they have been transmitted to our day, were never spoken in the Roman Senate. They were compositions after the fact. The splendid beginning of the first of the Catiline orations was never heard by public audience. They were composed as exercises by the great pleader, and were part of those exercitations of which he tells us that they were the stepping-stones to his splendour, and secrets of his power. The orations of Chesterfield, Walpole, and Pitt, so famous in the school-books, were, many of them, produced by the classic pen of Johnson, and first appeared in the *Gentleman's Magazine.*

There is, again, the method of meeting the demands of the pulpit by the plan of depositing in the memory the whole of the discourse intended to be delivered, sentence by sentence, and paragraph by paragraph. As this matter is most important, and one on which it is hardly competent to give any deliverance that would suit the peculiar tendencies of every modification of intellect, it will be necessary to say a few words regarding it: a plan, we believe, more generally adopted than what is imagined—adopted as long as the mind sustains the tension essential to its success. It is for us now to say a few words on its nature and its effects.

The memory is that power by which we recall to the mind past events, or past reminiscences, or past thoughts. It has been given for the purposes of daily life. We may also lay up in this storehouse which nature has fabricated, a number of the words which, in their collective capacity, embody the playful images of fancy or results of thinking. This power is faithful to its office, and is enabled to discharge its proper functions, but may suffer rather from minuteness of effort than magnitude of effort. Ideas which it has entertained may be recalled, though the vividness of their first visits cannot be commanded. Words themselves, as well as ideas, may be remembered, though, perhaps, in the best and most healthy exercise of this power, it is some idea, unconsciously operating, which restores the word when we want it. In forming a sentence, the subordinate ideas are never in the mind. But that words are connected with fancy and clearness of mental vision, is evinced by the fact that force of expression and nice selection of words are in proportion to splendour of imagination and brilliancy of conception.

If mere words, therefore, should ever take, before the mind, the place of thoughts, we would be inclined to say that the mind was rather in a state of debility than strength. Thus if we say, "All the rivers in the world run into the sea," the substantial information conveyed is one proposition; but should the word *river* conjure up in the mind the figure of a river, or the *world* of an immense sphere, or the *ocean* that mighty collection of waters which we designate by that name, we should then say that the mind was domineered over by mere words instead of sentiments. Words, it ought to be remembered, are not to be the objects of the mind. They are ideas which are the objects of the mind. And words merely serve the purpose of communicating thought and feeling. The whole subject is carefully examined by E. Burke in Treatise "On the Sublime and Beautiful."

The mind, in short, ought to be kept as free as possible from the influence of mere words. But if mere words be reposited in the memory, there will be a danger of the loss of that inventiveness by which images, ideas, thoughts, present themselves involuntarily on the mental field; and thus, that

the mighty and comprehensive intellect might be reduced to a
state in which it could retain words much better than ideas.
One fact is certain, according to our hypothesis, that the capacity
for seizing, comprehending, and delighting in grand description
and sublimity of thought or sentiment, and the power of retaining words in the memory, are in reverse ratio to one another.
Originality and exuberance of mind cannot co-exist with mere
power of retaining words. It is an axiom, then, that if the
power of remembering words be increasing, the power of originating ideas must be diminishing.

We hold, nevertheless, that could it be practised with im-
punity, the best sermons would be those which were first, with
ardour and care, committed to paper, and then transferred most
exactly, every word occupying its precise place, to the tablet of
memory. This exercise, it is evident, would include excogitation
or thinking out the subject, and complete inscription on paper
from beginning to end, and, lastly, engraving, as it were, on
memory word by word and sentence by sentence till, by this
process, the mind was so moved that it could not only deliver
the first ideas, but the words in which they were conceived.

We are not sure but that some minds may be so happily
constituted that this process is to them one of great ease. As
they describe the course they are to take, words may make so
indelible impression that thoughts will be remembered in the
very words in which they first occurred or were perceived by the
mind. We are not, however, to consider those peculiar mental
formations, but our remarks must be for those who present the
general and ordinary mental characteristics.

To minds, however, of a reflective turn, it would, we believe,
be the prostitution of all their powers; the utter extinction of
all the noble aspirations which belong to them; the total
destruction of their capacity for doing work in the lofty region
of abstract meditation. We are not able to form an exact
estimate of a process which we affirm to be so deleterious, as
we are reasoning on what we assume to be the nature or, if we
might so speak, the composition of the mind of man. In the
case of the celebrated French preacher, whose sermons are
such noble specimens of the eloquence of the pulpit, and were

F

ofttimes the cause of serious misgiving, anxious enquiry, if not
of real conversion, to the French nobility, it is said to have
been this mistake which he made of committing his addresses
to memory which, when he was made bishop, deprived the
pulpit of an eloquence so useful and touching. His mind turned
into a receptacle of mere words, lost the beautiful power which
conceives and comprehends thought, and after some time the
powerful genius, arrested by mere words, and seeking painfully
after them, was deprived of that animation which is the chief
excellency of eloquence.

The young preacher might, indeed, if the religious community to which he gave his services regarded everything else
with intolerance, venture on the complete mastering of one or two
sermons, so as to conserve in his memory the exact language in
which they were written. But he should endeavour to make
such slavery temporary, and as soon as possible betake himself
to another method. He ought to be mindful never to allow words
to usurp the place of ideas, and remember that the originating,
the creating faculty is to be preserved in unimpaired integrity,
and by no means to be lowered to a conservatory of words,
instead of a discoverer of ideas. He is to guard against such
a perversion of mind, and is to remember that it is his part not
only "to keep his heart with all diligence," but keep his intellect
with all diligence. He is, if we might so speak, to economize
his faculties; to preserve his intellect in all its youthful exuberance and strength, susceptible to the impressions of that
loveliness so visibly stamped on the works of creation, as well as
to the power of those moral emotions which are raised in the
soul by witnessing some act of injustice or benefaction of kindness, forbearance of patience, the inflexibility of righteousness,
or the charm of those moral emotions by which man is
distinguished.

But the less he can render it consistent with the sincere
discharge of undertaken duty to exercise his mind as a container
of mere language, the better it will be found to be for his own
interests, and, we believe, for the good of the community to
which he belongs. A great divine has said, speaking of the
puerile partialities which obtain among the community—

"Among these, we would remark its puling and fantastic antipathy to all the visible symptoms of written preparation in the pulpit; and its jealousy of all doctrine that is uttered in any other than the current phraseology; and its sensitive recoil from such innovations of outward reform as might simplify or improve any of the services of the church; and its appetite for length and loudness and wearisome occasions; and other puerilities, which have made it appear an utterly weak and contemptible thing in the eye of many a scornful observer." Again he says— "One reason becomes manifest why, on the part of clergymen, the mere whimsies of popular feeling ought not to be complied with, and that, between favourite preachers and their doting admirers, such a spectacle should never be held out, as that of servile indulgence on the one side, and weak, trifling, senseless conceits of taste and partiality on the other." Again—"If it be grievous to observe the demand of the people about frivolities of no moment, it is still more grievous to behold the deference which is rendered thereto by the fearful worshippers at the shrine of popularity. It is a fund of infinite amusement to lookers-on, when they see, in this interchange of little minds, how small matters can become great, and each caprice of the popular fancy can be raised into a topic of gravest deliberation. It were surely better that Christian people reserved their zeal for essentials, and that Christian teachers, instead of pampering the popular taste into utter childishness, disciplined it by a little wholesome resistance into an appetite at once manly, rational, and commanding."

We have now but to remark on the last method which may be adopted in the delivery of sermons—a method held in great disrespect by the generality of people, who in some way entertain the notion that it is done with such facility. I refer to the reading of sermons. An illiberal suspicion does attach to the readers of their sermons, as if they, above all, were exposed to the temptation of adopting a discourse which was not their own; than which nothing could, when examined, be more unlikely. We venture to say that the man who would go to the pains of copying a discourse from some antiquated volume, would also have the power of composing one. Nor is there one who should be less exposed to the suspicion of laying claim to writings not his own, than the man who brings his written preparation, and exposes his pages honestly to the view of all, nor seeks to mask his design by a compromise between composed and extemporaneous language.

Indeed, so prejudicial to the mental faculties do we believe the habit of making sermon-preparation an act of memory, collecting again the words in which the mind has produced its thoughts, that we wish that every one endowed with a fine taste for the labour of writing, and withal an energetic manner of reading what he wrote, were possessed of the courage, rather than adopt a hurtful alternative, of coming forward with what in his closet he had produced. There is nothing at all to be condemned in the proceeding. If he is conscious of the ability to read with power; if his bias is strongly in favour of written preparation, we see not how he is obliged to conceal or ignore the rich capacity which nature has conferred upon him. Those whose only idea of a sermon is, that it is a popular harangue, infinitely divided, and lasting a wearisome length of time—distinguished by great vocal ability—its language not very select or very elegant—they may be annoyed, and their preconceptions may meet with something mightily offensive. But is the young minister, ardently devoted to his Master's cause, and feeling there is one way he can present the mysteries of the faith in all their magnificence, in language and style becoming so solemn intimations, is he to render his ability in vain, lest he may act in the face of unreasoning prejudice, disgraceful to literature and cultivation, and which, we have no doubt, has been a great means of rendering useless a large portion of the talent of many churches, and withdrawing from the cause of Christian literature, eloquence and abilities which might have refuted the adversary, and exalted the Christian argument and cause?

Some years ago a book was composed, we think by a minister of religion, in which a custom of exercitation was greatly advocated and recommended. It was to choose some subject, or take some verse of Scripture, and unfold, explain, elucidate, and enlarge on the subject or verse, as long as the mind offered thought and conception. This is evidently within the power of all to try.

It is an exercise not exposed to the glare of publicity; and yet, in the secrecy of the chamber, as much care might be taken of directness of argument, and beauty of illustration, and eloquence of diction, as if surrounded by a tasteful and intellectual auditory. It is true the audience is the addition of a new and rather confusing element. But it is not to be supposed that he would be less fitted by this exercise for confronting a most critical body of hearers. And we venture to say, that if this mode of evoking or soliciting the mental powers were generally practised, the preparations of the pulpit would increase in worth and dignity, in brilliancy and copiousness of conception, instead of being confined to the narrow circle of a few truths and their never-varying round of argument and description.

Preaching has, indeed, been confined to a very contracted range of subjects. A few points of theology have been its only material. These become trite and familiar by repetition. It would also seem as if theology were something disannexed from terrestrial ethics, or any thing affecting the economy of the universe; as if it were some kind of mechanical doctrine, not receding and not advancing, obtaining complete development in a single age, holding in contempt the aids of science, insisting on the position that the knowledge of a few doctrines is a sufficient security against the anger of Heaven's law, though the believer of these doctrines were by no means a model of terrestrial morality, but might be the incarnation of a great deal not recon-cilable with principle or piety. General theology has sometimes adopted the tone, as if earthly virtue, the grandeur of generosity and softness of benevolence, or loveliness of self-sacrifice or affection, had no place nor rank in her dogmata.

This idea of such a theology, too much dwelt on, has led people sometimes to think that all obligation was cancelled; that they were constrained by no self-respect, pleased with no lofty sense of unsullied integrity; that the utterance or admission of a few charmed symbols had the effect of making them righteous without effort, virtuous without morality, and could endow them with a passport to heaven, without any of the attributes without which we cannot enter there.

We know not why it is that any topic, fitted by its treatment to enlarge our views of the Most High, or set forth the immensity of His vast creation, or to cast an illustration on His attributes, or impress with the loveliness of virtue, should, as if bearing a stigma upon it, be disqualified by a tacit consent from forming a topic for the expositions of the chair of the Christian instructor. Sure we are that no such topic is excluded from the book whence he derives his evangelical materials. The Bible presents them all, and insists on them all. If Christianity has her handmaids, her auxiliaries, why not seek to gain those who can see their beauty without seeing that of the system which advances them? If infidelity can be deprived of its supports, and they be shown to be the genuine supports of the evangelical system, why by any means exclude—why not admit them to the honours they deserve? and instead of making the pulpit a confined and contracted theatre for the exposition of precise and scholastic systems, why not widen it out into a platform of usefulness, fitted to commend itself, by attainments and knowledge, "to every man's conscience," and taking into its ample embrace a vast and neglected class, unconsidered and uncared for in the present system of its lessons and its teachings?

CHAPTER VII.

AN anecdote is related in the "Life of Demosthenes," that being asked what was the first requisite of the orator, he said, "Action"; what was the second, he said, "Action"; and what the third, "Action," still. If this story be correct, it introduces us to the secret of his success and immortality. Of this quality Cicero says, that nothing is better fitted to find a way into men's minds, to affect, move, and bend them whither we wish. It is impossible to attach too much importance to a quality which ought to accompany language spoken before a public audience.

Now we come to what, instead of action, we may speak of as delivery. Nothing is more common than to say that a man has good matter, a profound intellect, good language, but that from the effect of all these his bad delivery makes such deductions as to render his matter valueless, his intellect useless, his language tame and ineffectual. The possession of what is designated good delivery must, therefore, be considered of great importance; indeed, of the very first importance, as without it all is vain. This arises from the fact that a general audience is more impressed by what they see than what they hear—that vehemence of manner is more impressive than fineness of language. Indeed the word which means in our language to act, meant in the Latin tongue to plead as well as to act; and when we remember that the ambassador of Christ beseeches men, with all the earnestness of the most affecting entreaty, "to be reconciled to God," and consider that all the ardour of the most strenuous entreaty is not enough to have effect on men reluctant to think of heaven, or take the matter of their reconcilement into consideration, we shall understand that if there be not all the violence of a personal effort in representing the cause and pleading the cause, not a soul may be reclaimed from darkness and brought into the lustrous effulgence of "the marvellous light."

This delivery is all the more important, as it gives an idea of something actually done—of action, which means literally something effected. This is eminently needful, as it will be remembered from our previous remarks that the minister's work consists rather in persuading than enlightening. It is more on the heart than the head. The emotions are his object. The impressible nature of man is his object. If he can produce good resolves, fervent aspirations, the love of his Heavenly Benefactor, determination on the side of principle and truth— if he can subvert the strongholds of unbelief and error—this is just what he ought to accomplish. This is what the earthly "daysman" ought to have before his eyes continually. His high position is between God and man, like Phinehas. Whatever realizing power he is endowed with to understand or be moved by the full force of this conception, yet every minister of the Gospel is, in one sense, an intercessor with men to accept the terms which Heaven's condescension presents, and so to possess their minds with the necessity and nature of salvation as to make them Christians.

No matter how sincere the speaker be, or how much the torch of divine love burns in his own bosom, yet if we see him deliver a quiet essay on some momentous subject, as redemption, death, perdition, eternity; if none of the fervour of his own nature be exhibited; if there be no *action*, no appearance of work done, how is it possible that a body of people, strangers to the wrestlings or workings of his own soul, can gather an impression from what is said? Nay, so very important is this matter of delivery, that a sermon in an unknown tongue, and yet still accompanied with the eloquence of gesture and action, would, by the very force of manner, be more effective than a sermon in a tongue with which we were familiar, if it still were destitute of these important accessories.

But where there is real passion there must be action. Where there is a burning ardour there must be an exterior which permits the ardour to shine through into an impressive manifestation. In proportion to the agitations of the internal are the movements of the external. The very eyes undergo a change. The features of the countenance are affected, not dis-

torted. The frame, without being convulsed, is made to respond
to the sentiment. The arms are made to represent the action
and exhibit the sentiments without the absurdity of preposterous
attitudes. The frame is so organized that there is a certain
natural harmony. Intense feeling demands corresponding
action ; and gesture keeps company with pathos, or passion, or
objurgation, or menace, or even with description.

Some topics may be expanded or elucidated; and in doing
this, action is not absolutely essential to the effect. Thus a
geological dissertation or disquisition on the principles of
morality may have sufficient attraction for an audience, independent of peculiarities of delivery. What is merely for the
gratification of the intellect—that about which feeling is indifferent—does not demand any exhibition which may move,
agitate, or impel. The heart is not interested in the matter of
geological theories, or strata, or imbedded and now extinct
tribes, which one time browsed on a herbage as gigantic and
wonderful as themselves, and roamed the denizens of a world
unblessed by man, and where civilization had not yet put forth
its powers. The sage philosopher is only addressing the intellect.

But how different from this are the subjects which furnish
to the theologian the domain over which he expatiates! It
is impossible to conceive of themes whose very essence is
fitted to exercise all the faculties of our nature more than do
those which the Bible sets before us. We cannot conceive how,
without all the pathos of entreaty, the vehement ardour of
one evidently himself elevated with a sense of their extreme
importance, any lasting good can be done. This demand is no
popular caprice. As human nature is constituted, it is a most
allowable and reasonable demand. It cannot be arraigned as a
vulgar prejudice. Nor is it at all worthy of the contempt with
which it may, in some quarters, be regarded. The man who
has felt the grace, or estimated properly the meaning of the
Gospel message, cannot but be moved; and for the people to
demand the show of interest, ardour, entreaty, is to do what they
ought to do.

As people become more enlightened, as their minds are
more developed, they will require less the benefit of an art which

may be said to have reached its perfection in a comparatively unenlightened period of the world's history. As light advances, the perturbations of passion may recede or diminish. Yet though this might be the case with regard to subjects on which passion was interested in a less cultivated age, yet it is to be questioned if it be so with Christianity. It is to be questioned if, when fervour departs on the subject of Christianity, *it* has not departed along with the fervour. The latter may mark our interest in the former. The two may co-exist and be contemporary. It is not an ephemeral system we are dealing with. It is not for a day. Its themes, where it is properly understood, are vested with as great importance and sublimity as when first its light irradiated the darkness of the globe. The doings of ancient factions and sects may be untombed from the dreary recesses of the past, and may be related without evoking a particle of that interest which at one time distinguished opinions which enlisted all the ardour of love or rancour of vengeance. But what heart is moved on the wars of the Roses or the boisterous dissensions of an age passed away? Its sentiments are now extinct. We can no more be engaged in the interest of their parties than in the defence of the armed and frowning strongholds that maintained them. But a divine system never passes away. Not one jot or tittle of the law can be abolished. It is not for one age, but every age. It will flourish amid the most different terrestrial systems. It professes not to favour one particular clique of political believers. It is for man as man, and not as politician.

Tameness of manner may be here charged as infidelity to the cause. This, at least, is the popular view of the matter. And as it is the majority who are supposed to be interested in this grand scheme, it is as well to leave them without any excuse, by bringing every faculty to bear with all its might on the subject whose cause is advocated. Let the solemn thought that he is endeavouring to awaken the dormant and earthbound soul to the grandest of concerns; that he is engaged in the work of opening an avenue of access for the entering of the Gospel; that he is, if the Gospel be true, actually in conflict with a dire and unrelenting Satanic agency, which is doing everything to deaden and counteract all the efforts of the disciples of Jesus; let all this endue the standard-bearers of the cross with fortitude, and evoke new force and new enthusiasm in the cause.

With regard to the marks of delivery which would seem to be most popular, we might say, first of all, that it ought to agree with, and be produced by the sentiment. It should not rise higher; it should not descend lower than the subject. To see a minister pronounce a discourse perfectly at his ease, and in a composed and quiescent manner, which ought to stimulate him to energy and enthusiasm, is an exhibition which pronounces rather unfavourably on his mode of preparation. To see one pronounce a discourse on grand and ennobling themes, without being stirred by them himself, shows that it is with him a mere effort of memory; that any emotion would be to his total discomposure, or that emotion is not awakened by them. If it is the first, he has entered on an ill-chosen and rather inadequate mode of preparation. If it be the second, he has not as yet engaged the whole heart in the cause, or perhaps is possessed of intellectual clearness rather than intensity of feeling. When the manner is produced by the sentiment, there is no danger of emotion being displayed when it is out of place, or of the sublimest sentiments being spoken without action. We have heard it told of a minister of the Gospel who, in making marks and directions on his sermon, was in the habit of planting such notes as these along the margin of his manuscript—"earnest here," "be pathetic here," "animated here." When, however, he became older, he could hardly remember the side directions and composition both, so he became pathetic to tears where there was nothing to move, and was not pathetic enough where the sentiment would have excused them. There was thus something strange and rather unbecoming in the display of emotion where the subject did not require it.

If any one, interested in the direction about delivery being produced by the particular sentiment, compare together Othello's address to the senators, defending himself for carrying off Brabantio's daughter, and Satan's address to the sun in Milton, he will perceive a great contrast between the calm, unimpassioned address of the Moor of Venice and the wild agitations, the fierce and terrible gestures, and the despair of a great and reprobate spirit who knows that he will never reascend to happiness; that the recklessness of chaos and the element of evil will be his good, and the scene of his future history. We cannot conceive of one blessed with sensibilities reading these extracts in the same manner. The one is the address of a courtier. The other is the utterance of the fell and terrible author of evil, like a scorpion stinging himself to anguish and rage by the gloomy complexion of his own fierce and foreboding meditations. In the one, it is the individual using all the blandness of conciliation to propitiate his judges, and appease their rage. In the other, it is the ebullition of a sad, despairing, and fallen spirit, in solitude and alone, giving vent to the anguish which devours him. Motion and gesture must accompany the sentiment.

Again, of all kinds of delivery, it is required for their best effect that they be free and animated. This might, perhaps, include celerity and dispatch, which is most important. A slowly uttered discourse would appear to possess this advantage, that it gave time to consider each distinct clause as it is delivered. It has, strange to say, an opposite effect—that of allowing the listeners to attend as they please to any particular speculation of their own mind. Their thoughts, instead of being confused, are only aroused by some degree of rapidity. This seems to be necessary for giving an address power and bearing on those who hear it. It has the good result of preventing anything else—any other process of thought—from being conducted during the time it is delivered. It disposts out of the olden habit of lethargy. It is not impossible that the rapid movement of one mind may set in motion other minds; and this is just what is necessary to stimulate and awaken the power of thought, to make human beings think for themselves—think rightly and with effect. It is not likely that one mind, anxious for the propriety of its own processes, advancing every step with tediousness and labour, and having to premeditate the fitness of every word before it is spoken, will put other minds into life, energy, and motion—will stir the hidden fountain of thought, or hurry auditors onward to grand convictions, fitted to work a change in their hearts and understandings.

Longinus, in his treatise on *to hupsos*, the sublime, informs us that it consists in the power which anything written has in hurrying us out of ourselves—surprising or transporting us by celerity or by imaginary descriptions. The word *transport*, the same almost as *ecstasy*, means carrying us beyond ourselves, and therefore to something else; making words and sentences tell or bear with such an impression on us that we are made to see, to feel, to consider the substantial shapes and forms which these words and sentences signify. As the grandest instance of the sublime, this great teacher notices Homer absorbing his reader, collecting his energies, showing him scenes in words and battles in lines; surprising by his vividness of description, his metaphor, his simile; arousing the powers and inflaming the heart by the velocity of his own progress. Animating is actually imparting a spirit, a soul, a power to what by itself is without life or power. If the sinner is to be hurried out of the current of his own impetuous and wayward fancies, it must be by a current at least equally rapid. If the herald of the Gospel wish to carry him forward on a new current that he may land him in a new region, he must make its rapidity proportioned to his object. His object is to discompose, shatter, destroy, change, divert old habits of thought, and make them new. This can be done only by a rapid and impetuous motion given to his own eloquence. It may thus absorb into the current the minds of other men, and this, in all likelihood, would become the grand instrument of winning Christians to the faith.

But, again, the minister of the Gospel should, withal, be natural. Independently of rules, there is something in nature which it is difficult to disguise or to change. One whose mind it is hard to move, whose conceptions are destitute of vividness, who has no emotions, or ones not easily aroused, will never become like the ardent, impetuous being whose whole soul is habitually aware of the presence of great principles, and can never consider any question without reference to them. Rules and directions will be of small avail with either of these natures. The one requires a stimulus, and we know not how it is to be imparted. The other no sooner turns the mental aspect on a subject, than it arises before him without apparent effort in all its dimensions, and varieties, and applications. His survey of it is not by stages, but, as it were, by penetration—intuition. There is a native difference between the eagle towering over the landscape and the organism which sees only what is in its immediate field of view.

But to adopt a manner which is not natural, to subdue the impetuosity of inborn feeling down to calm and unemotional quiescence, or to act as if one was inflated with animal spirits and a buoyancy not belonging to them, is not only not beneficial, but positively injurious. To exhibit zeal and interest where they are not innate, is showing more than is felt, and can hardly be equal to the task of creating feeling in others. However, the naturally tranquil and self-possessed, if they cannot stir emotion, may be enabled to acquire graces which may render their efforts pleasing, and may do much, by new endeavours, by a change of studies, or keeping great and affecting objects before their minds, to impart to their subjects new interest; so that, if they are true to their own natures, they will be enabled properly to discharge the functions of persuasion and impression. We place it to another account than any lack of natural sensibility that the efforts of the pulpit are sometimes ineffectual, that the essays are devoid of what is fitted to affect the heart or inform the mind; and we have reason to believe that in the course of our suggestions as much may have been said as will prove a warning against what might be destructive of their full efficiency, or retard the advance of that great cause in the interests of which they are employed.

There is one advantage in being natural, that it assists to do away with those conventionalities and set forms in religion which destroy its spirit. A more fatal blow could not be aimed at religion than to act as if it consisted in what was fashionable; and that if some uninteresting detail, delivered in a voice and manner which too plainly declare that the heart is not in the work, be listened to on the appointed day, all the claims of religion are met and completely liquidated. Feeling is considered, in one class of society, to savour of what is unmannerly. The principle has also, in some way, insinuated itself into the church. And the manifestation of any inward disturbance is thought to be redolent of Methodism or fanaticism; just as if, on the principle that Christianity were literally what it professes to be, its themes were not fitted to come to the heart in a way at once convincing and affecting; just as if, with subjects of themselves so commanding and touching, the individual who, while they were sounding in his ears, kept them at the farthest distance, and viewed them with the glance of unimpassioned coolness, were the best Christian; just as if it were not display-ing Nature's grandeur, and none of her weakness, to have a heart so tuned and fashioned as that all the chords of its moral nature responded to every representation, either of heavenly benevolence, or a suffering Mediator, or a beseeching God, which was naturally fitted to thrill and to influence them.

No one, as we at least apprehend, could consider the amazing actualities of the Christian faith, as it is described in the New Testament, without a feeling and impression from them. To a pure and unbiassed nature, the sight of a good and righteous man suffering unheard-of calamities, and, at last, to forward some great interest of philanthropy, submitting to a shameful and cruel martyrdom, must be affecting in the extreme. We cannot understand, even on the supposition that Christ was a human being of great benevolence and unyielding principle of honour and justice, how any one could apprehend such a truth and yet be unconscious of an interest in Him as the first expounder of principles which never before had been heard of. But a divine system goes farther than this. It is not satisfied with such a concession. Its pretensions are far loftier. Its disciples must go beyond this. As far as Christianity is con-cerned, they believe nothing, when they believe this; for its lofty declaration is that Christ "came from God and went to God."

It might be supposed, therefore, to have every tendency to create a delivery at once animated and natural when the mind is frequently engaged in contemplating such subjects. This exercise might be the only one demanded to give a delivery which would possess some characteristic at least of those mentioned. We cannot understand but that some sentiments might call forth the right and corresponding gesture and voice fitted to give them all the influence they can possess. Such

expressions as, "Behold Him nailed to the accursed tree—
see Him suspended there for the sin of the world;" or, "Hark
to that voice of agony! He utters His last cry. He bows
the head, He groans, and dies," are sufficient to produce the
corresponding action. Ejaculations like these are fitted more
forcibly to interest the mind of the hearer than a didactic essay
never rising above one uniform level, and adorned with all the
learning of the scholar. Exclamation will thus have a most
important place in not only producing right gestures, but in
creating interest. Could a preacher, his eyes intently fixed in
surprise and wonder, as if they were settled on the very scene
he was describing, utter the exclamation, "But who is this I
behold in company of the vilest malefactors, nailed to the fatal
tree? It is He by whom the worlds were made and He dies for
the sins of man!" it would be more calculated to set open the
flood-gates of sympathy, to induce a sensibility, and perhaps give
an impulse on the path heavenward, than the most philosophic
disquisition which the lessons of the Academy could enable the
minister to prepare.

It was, in a great measure, by depicting the harrowing
torments of the impenitent, as well as describing the glories of
paradise, and making his hearers see the whole by the aid of
inimitable gestures, and probably inimitable language, it was in
this way that Whitefield not only acquired the greatest degree
of popularity, but perhaps wrought the greatest amount of usefulness. A nature so sensitive and affectionate, with conceptions
so exceedingly vivid, that what was related in a book was enacted
over again by his intellect, cannot be imparted; but it may be
good to know that the source of his gestures was not the prescription of any teacher of public speaking, but his own heart.
Of him it was said, that so flexible was his voice that, by itself,
it was fitted to produce any emotion, and communicate it to
others. His whole system was incessantly on the stretch by
reason of emotions and agitations within. And "now, sinner,"
he would say, "I must put on the black cap. I must pronounce
the sentence of condemnation on you, and that sentence is—
Depart, ye cursed, into everlasting fire." We are not at all
amazed that His ministrations were awakening and useful.

Voice is the sound in which, by articulated vocables, sense and mind are conveyed, by a ready channel of communication, from one human being to another, or from one to a multitude; and must therefore be held, in pronouncing a discourse, to be very important; so much so, that it is, when possessed in all its power of modulation, a talent in itself, which may sometimes compensate for want of judgment or of learning. To preserve those parts on which the voice depends, or by which it is formed, in their integrity, must be essential in one used to address audiences in public. To do so, the parts ought to be properly and daily exercised, and this exercise has one benefit; for whereas other kinds of exertion may debilitate the intellect, this exercise aliments, nourishes, and strengthens the mind. The exercise of reading aloud in a manner as expressive as possible, and with intonations and changes of voice answering to the subject, must be held to be one fitted to effect the purpose of inflating the lungs, and giving strength to all the parts that come into use in speaking. Nor should one kind of reading be kept to, nor one tone persisted in. Perhaps dialogue, in which two parties address one another, and may be supposed to adopt a tone grave or gay, careless or severe, tragic or comic, is the best fitted for this exercise. While the reading of sermons of the highest class for language, sentiment and style, with remarks of one's own interspersed, must be the exercise which best befits the minister who wishes to grace and commend the grandest truths.

That many pieces be committed to memory, and delivered again by an effort of memory, is, we believe, pernicious to the mind, and probably injurious to the important organ on which the mind seems to depend. The speaker ought, in what he terms recitation, to have the book before him from which he reads. We say this from the consideration, that we hold the faculty by which he is trained to see and admire the beautiful, sublime, and elegant, in his author, and is enabled to grasp the scope of the whole, is much more valuable than the mere memory, in which he may deposit, by most laborious and, as we hold it, injurious repeatals, the great bulk of his author, word for word. For this reason, also, we have condemned, as likely injurious, the practice of committing many sermons to the memory.

G

Some qualities will be indispensable to the voice, to fit it for the just enunciation of a discourse. It ought to be loud. It ought to be in volume. It ought to be able to express degrees of pathos and feeling. Loudness will convey it to a fitting distance, according to the demand for it. It must not, however, be disagreeably loud—rolling in one continuous discharge on the heads of the listeners—conveying not ideas, but inflicting suffering. A voice of this kind, where the orator vociferates without moderation or judgment, is fitted to offend, and connects an unpleasant association with the message he is delivering. Besides, there is a way of emitting the voice in such violent disharges as that the words themselves are lost in the sound, and the hearer is conscious of nothing but a noise.

The voice must be, moreover, in volume. It may be loud, and even distressing by loudness, and yet not be in volume. It may also have volume, as we think, independent of loudness. Mere loudness is just noise made by the organ. Volume would seem to be its proper emission from the organs of speech, so as to produce an agreeable flow over the hearers. This may be secured by attending to certain rules, such as opening the mouth for its proper formation, and inflating the lungs for its continuance in a right and adequate supply. When the voice is emitted in proper volume, it may be diminished in mere loudness, as volume is more pleasing than noise. There ought to be an effort to make the voice take its departure from the mouth when it is sufficiently formed. It is owing to neglect of this rule that many speakers, notwithstanding their noise, seem rather to hold their voice imprisoned in the mouth. Their utterance has noise, but wants volume. It is never made agreeably to affect the ears of the people who are listening and trying to collect "the meaning of the voice."

The voice ought to be modulated to express all varieties of feeling and each degree of pathos. It is naturally fitted to do so. The tones which belong to any one voice are so many as to exceed calculation. And yet we might suppose, from the kind of use which is made of it in public, we would fancy that every man was gifted with a voice which never underwent any change of tone. This arises from want of exercise. The extreme and wonderful flexibility of the human voice—its adaptation to convey every variety of meaning and all kinds of emotion which can affect the mind—can be perceived by those accustomed to read aloud. Whether it be irony, satire, ridicule, affection's breathings, the terrible ebullitions of anger, the deep and awful mutterings of revenge, the painful tortures of jealousy, the moanings of sorrow, agonizing exclamations of despair, or the beseeching entreaties of good-will, nature has furnished man with an organ more expressive of them all than any instrument ever fabricated by his hands or devised by his invention.

But it is not less essential that the voice be distinct. "If the trumpet issue an uncertain sound, who shall prepare himself to the battle?" Every word should fall on the ear, not only with the amount of modulation which belongs to it, but with perfect distinctness. If the leading word in a sentence be mispronounced, or imperfectly articulated, the sentence is disfigured, if not lost. Language is, no doubt, formed to present a kind of cadence. But if a syllable be dropt, or the last portion of a word receive less attention than the first; if each word is not made to carry, by the ear, its own impression to the mind, all the elegance of diction suffers a proportionate loss, and the whole composition becomes like a house out of which its materials are extracted, here and there, and which, though as a finished edifice it may delight the eye, yet, now no longer presenting the appearance of such edifice, no longer attracts the beholder. Every word has its office to perform. "And's," "the's," "now's," "but's"—those cementing particles which fasten the whole, without which it would be detached, unconnected—though apparently unworthy of attention, yet show more palpably the movement and processes of the thoughts than any other words. As these may be delicately handled and made most impressive by the toiling orator, so they ought to be distinctly pronounced. Their smallness is not insignificance. Some affect their removal from composition. But such erasures from the language are not to be admired, as they are found scattered in great profusion on the surface of every advanced and cultivated language throughout the world.

CHAPTER VIII.

LITERATURE NOT HOSTILE TO RELIGION. SELF-DISCIPLINE. LABOUR
AMONG THE POOR, &c.

IT has been frequently observed that when those preliminary
studies which are regarded as necessary to qualify for any
profession have been sufficiently pursued for that purpose, and
when the young candidate for the worldly competency has been
rewarded by success, he then treats these studies as the ambitious
man does the ladder by which he has attained to the height of
his power or popularity—he turns his back upon them. These
stepping stones, which have been deemed indispensable to his
entering on his office, are thought no longer necessary once he
has entered on it. The office is generally looked upon as a
period of ease, only to be attained by an apprenticeship of labour
and pursuit. If he have the requisite qualifications, whatever
pains he may have been at in acquiring them, a compensation
is supposed to exist in the repose, the ceremony, and perquisites
of office. By this kind of estimate, it follows either that the
gradations of advancement, and the ordeal he has to pass to
obtain the right to exercise his profession, have been more
essential as a kind of ceremonious and understood admittance to
his profession, than essential in the nature of the thing itself,
or that the candidate might be charged with injustice to those
studies by his present neglect. Has he been emancipated from
the degrading drudgery of a state of dependent pupilage? Has
he obtained a deliverance from a nauseated process, to endure
which the expected honours or benefits of his calling could alone
have lured him? Has the sole fascination of his studies been
the expected pleasure or emoluments in which they have
terminated? Have all his length of service, and the nights of
vigil, in which he spent his midnight oil in the laborious preparations of solution, and essay, and of made-out responses to
profound and professorial interrogatories, been seasons in which
he was cheered along his self-denying career by the perspective
of the reward and the scene of leisurely repose? Does he fancy
that he is now released from taking a single additional step in

the enlargement of the field of thought? Does he congratulate himself that he is for ever delivered from painstaking and imposed self-denial, and all that "weariness of the flesh," allied, by the wisest of men, with much study; and, a sentiment no doubt joined in by the scions of a degenerate age, prepared to enjoy the honour without adding to the grand products of their severely toiling forefathers? If this be the idea of the candidate, we can assure him that whatever repose he has earned, it is inglorious, and his labours will never be honoured of man, nor receive the applause of his own conscience.

It is essential that the delusion should be removed, if it should have gained a lodging-place in any bosom, that all those preparatory accomplishments in literature, science, and art, are useless; and, now that the end of the journey is reached, are of no more service. It would certainly be no small deduction from the moral lustre of any profession, that neither labour nor thought—no literary tastes or preparations—are essential for its proper discharge; and much more, if the office be that of one who, when all adventitious and conventional phrases are removed, simply addresses himself to the human intellect, and is supposed to be engaged in the work of collecting and preparing argument and illustration, and considering the best forms and expressions in which he may pioneer his way to the heart and understanding. Surely no tacit intimation would be meant to be conveyed that, after all, the end of the study was the competency supposed to be attached to the profession to which it leads. And even if the specific studies which have prefaced his entrance on an important walk or field of occupation have been regarded as essential, while he was in the avenue which conducted to the full engagements of his employment, are there no specific studies, no vigils, no prolonged meditations, which are needful for the requisite adornment of the office itself? Indeed, to suppose that neither study nor mental labour were attached to a work, in which it seems to be the mind which, to all human seeming, is the great agent, were utterly to degrade and bring down from their lofty elevation all the departments of the office itself. The teacher of Christianity, properly recognized to be so for his scholarly accomplishments and academic tastes, has, at all events, entered on a new province of duty in which he may still render available a portion of that former learning which he has acquired, and may of "his spiritual things" impart such a tasteful and well-prepared abundance as will not cause him to experience a conscientious compunction, should he reap abundantly of "the carnal things" of the world. He will feel that he has a right to them, even that of unintermitted efforts to adorn his vocation. He will despise the "recompense of reward" that would come to him in any other way than that of an equivalent for the abundant labours of his own mind. He will feel that he has made a contract of pure equity, and not of sordid or gainful bartering, in which the profit is altogether on his own side and not on the side of a badly-cared for charge, where his flock, trying hard to excuse all his failings in duty, his neglect or want of circumspection, and even his more reprehensible qualities, without finding fault, are left to languish and pine away, untended and uncared for.

Designated to the work by the by no means impartial estimate of parental fondness; stimulated by friends and relatives, even in years when they are not competent to form a judgment or make a choice; sustained in their efforts by the looked-for comforts of a position with which, we know not for what reason, opulence and ease are connected in the common opinion, the youthful teachers, ere they have attained ripeness of judgment, have entered on duties of a most sacred nature. In these circumstances, it would not be reasonable to expect that the capricious partiality of parents, themselves urged, perhaps, by motives not very proper, could be directed to a right object. The youthful aspirant may have had his mind fixed, not by the sacredness, but the secularities of his office. It may have been represented as an office of comfort and well-to-do respectability, different wholly from the toils of handicraft or the anxieties connected with other situations. The ordinary association, which may take place in their thoughts, is that they are rearing their son for an office in which he will not be exposed to the cares, solicitudes, and harassing anxieties of a secular calling— an office not suffering from the mishaps of merchandize or little gains pitifully accumulated, in daily attendance on which the grandeur of higher aspirations is prostrated in the dust. It is not to be supposed that this fondness, not given very much to think of the path to the profession, but merely to look at it as they see it exemplified in the rich and flourishing congregation, the neat and comfortable manse or glebe-house, in the respect paid to the sacerdotal order, will make the best possible selection, or be very attentive to any object beyond the final success of their plan. Ambition thinks more of the success of its project than benefit to the world at large.

In these circumstances, it can hardly be expected that the enforced labours of the closet—labours conducted and carried forward in compliance with the wishes of near relatives—could, in every case, be in accordance with personal tendencies, or be carried beyond a certain period. Indeed, we are far mistaken if many, after their degrees and examinations, manifest a tendency to feast the eye again on the imagery of Homer or Virgil, to investigate the names of ancient places, to construe the page of Livy, or to awe the soul with the sons and daughters of the house of Pelops, as their vast misfortunes and terrible fates are enacted on the page of Euripides or Æschylus. Few, perhaps, wipe the dust off the volume containing the polished elegance of Cicero, or the terse and reiterated oratory of Demosthenes. And there dwells, not in a few, the impression that farther prosecution of such studies would not only not be useful, but quite derogatory from the dignity of a new office; that to pursue such labours longer would be a sore misspending of moments that might be devoted to a better purpose. Time passed in this way, though the amount of time would, among hours perhaps employed in no nobler pursuit, be nothing, would be regarded by some as lost—as wholly misspent—as irreparably gone, and gone, too, with an account not very much in favour of their being so employed. To dwell on the page of Tacitus, Suetonius, or Pliny, would be regarded as an appropriation of time to base and ignoble uses which might have been spent in nobler studies or worthier compositions.

In the vast empire of thought, the Scriptures may be said to occupy a position among productions which the human mind has created. The Bible has not emanated, it is true, from the mind the way other compositions have. Its Author was greater than man. However, "holy men" at least knew the words they were engaged in tracing on their parchment; they were cognizant at the time of certain processes of thought; they could read and explore the surface which they had filled with communications from on high. We are, indeed, greatly in the dark with regard to the operation of their own minds in receiving the revelation. We have no reason, however, to suppose that they were either unconscious or unintelligent at the moment, but in possession of their faculties: for although "moved by the Holy Ghost," yet it was still "holy men spake as they were moved."

But the very faculties of mind which lead to the sacred page are the faculties which lead to the pages of general literature. Not only so, but by the employment of the intellect, at certain seasons, on the subjects of ordinary learning, the volume of Inspiration receives a new illustration. Names, places, histories, events, customs, mentioned in the directory of our faith, would be utterly unknown and unintelligible, were it not that the excursions of distant travel have put us in possession of such a mass of delightful and convincing evidence, in the form of usages, ceremonies, dress, architecture, and agriculture, found to exist in eastern kingdoms at the present day. Indeed, the sincerity shines forth—the lineaments of convincing honesty which belong to the Word of the Eternal—the truth of miraculous events such as Creation, Apostacy, Deluge, or common events, ancient wars, and extinguished tribes, are all brought out into convincing manifestation by the agreement between what the mind of man has discovered and the plain and recorded narratives contained in the Scriptures.

But might it not be questioned, if they who viewed literature as, in some way, opposed to the interests of religion, properly understood the book which they profess to honour with pure and holy regards? The grand attraction of the Bible, in their eyes, is not, we presume, what is said of it, but what it contains. We should expect the devout admirers of the sacred books to be doers, busily employed in the work of meditation and reading, all spent over its alarming and affecting contents. We should expect that not a day in their lives, or a moment in the day, but would find them paying to these divine documents the homage they profess to entertain for them. Should, however, neglect or disregard be discovered on the part of a few, may it not be asserted that their love displays itself in panegyric more than investigation; in utterance more than in practice? We therefore affirm that they who, with profound veneration and with a zeal accompanied with knowledge, and with a resolve to bring out "hidden things kept secret from the foundation of the world," betake themselves to the volume which "makes wise the simple," will likewise betake themselves to the external volume of the Almighty's workmanship; to the investigations of science; to that advancing river of thought which, commencing in the first conception or incipient idea, has come down to our day, diffusing its beneficent waters over the landscape, and carrying happiness and delight on its waves.

The apophthegm of the ancient sage was that he disregarded nothing human; the fact of its being of man made it interesting to man. If this be so, it is perhaps more than folly—it is impiety—to regard with the glance of scorn those mighty movements of ancient thought; those mysterious workings of the olden intellect; those wonderful conjectures; that light; that dawning projected by a morn of mighty promise, which was about to merge into an era of blessing and of faith. It is true that the present is a time of superior light, though not, perhaps, of greater intellect; of more stupendous doings in art, and more laboured and careful experimenting in science. But every one at all blessed by vividness of conception or by fervent piety will be anxious to know by what onward degrees it was that the Omniscient mind has brought the world at large to its present state of advancement and civilization. He will not so centre his gaze on the present as to withdraw it from that vast intervening period in which toiling generations traversed the earth, and were, in the grand profile of their moral nature, not unlike the generations who have now taken their place, and who trample on the dust of departed glory. He must remember that students then plied their assiduous efforts to find out the Unknown, and ascertain the Infinite. He must remember that historians have recorded, in language that will never perish, the stirring events, commotions, changes, and progress of that distant age, and that orators then engaged, as now, in the exposition of mighty and eternal principles, in defence of injured innocence, or in denunciation of unjust and ambitious designs.

Nor would any attention given to such subjects as these be any detraction from the efficiency of evangelical clergymen. It is, indeed, in some quarters a reproach, whether deserved or not we do not know, to the pulpit, that other departments of knowledge are becoming, day by day, more interesting and attractive; that experimental science can reward its devotees by the splendour and magnitude of its discoveries; that geology itself is expanding into something like a science with laws and data; that philology, in the hands of a Max Muller, has been made to tell on the most momentous questions; but that the teachings of the pulpit are going into desuetude; that it has nothing wherewith to repay the attendance of the man of intellect and scientific pursuit on its lessons. It is our glory that the essential ideas which lie at the basis of Christianity can undergo no change, without the destruction of Christianity itself. Let the Divine Sonship be taken away, or the mighty and sin-atoning Oblation be changed into the death of a philosophic and noble-hearted martyr, or the sanctifying *Pneuma*, Spirit, be changed into some energy which pervades creation, and we know not how Christianity, as understood and expounded by Paul and John, can remain at all. These are its life-blood. To make the surrender of any of these first principles is to surrender the citadel itself.

But perhaps the whole subject might be so blended with other topics, and so commended by beauty of language, or elegance of style, or fervour of utterance, as to gain to itself the ardent worshippers at the shrine of science and progress. However, if it be a concession and not a duty, yet it would be a most graceful, and, we think, conciliatory and acceptable concession, if the man who engages in expounding the mysteries of the skies, would, at certain seasons, come down from the high altitudes of theology, and show that he, for one, does not disdain the attempt to make science the handmaid of religion; and if he can gain the ardent disciples of philosophy to the school of Christ, he will himself make timely excursions into the domain of literature or philosophy, and, by his scholarly habits and abilities, will remove a reproach which is more than half-deserved. This is becoming "all things to all men." Though philosophy were vain, and science were delusive, and literature disqualified the mind for the reception of religious truth, yet it were the part of a certain courtesy to diminish the contemptuous disdain sometimes entertained for them.

Science and religion are not, however, like parallel lines, each extending in the same direction, but destined never to meet. They are inclined at a certain angle to each other, and casting continual confirmation the one upon the other. The theological argument has been dwelt on by the finest intellects; and Christianity can reckon in the list of its defenders the best benefactors of their species. Paley, Butler, Chalmers, have laboured on the same field, and contributed largely to the Christian evidences, although their arguments have sometimes more of a negative than positive aspect. Infidelity has since assumed another mode of attack; and arguments, sufficient to have discomfited the stalwart champions of the infidelity of the beginning of this century, are no longer able to do so. The bowels of the earth are ransacked, and no longer can the geologist be answered by the former arguments. The earth has supplied unmistakable evidences of an unsurmised antiquity, and the busy intellect of a Miller or Lyell has not been deterred by any such respect for Revelation as not to try and find "what these things meant"—what the meaning is of disinterred relics of species now no longer known to exist, and what particular development of terrestrial economy has been marked by the appearance of a nobler animal, gifted with an aspect fixed on heaven, an intellect able to walk the vast amplitude of creation.

Now, indeed, is not the time for ministers of the Gospel to fall behind the pioneers of science, as if the mind of the age would not muster all its abilities to solve the enigma of creation, out of respect for articles of a creed or names by which they are supported. It is true that the teacher of Christianity may say, "I will set up the barriers of resistance against the intrusion of questions so perplexing and so ominous to the faith. I cannot be supposed to be at home on this field." It is doubtful, though, whether the Christian people would be satisfied to see their spiritual guides make a defence so lame and disastrous; and we think the time has come when to meet questions of this kind openly is to meet them judiciously, and to avert from the Christian doctrines such a blow, dealt to them by their very interpreters and friends.

Indeed, what with the ample authorship of classic lore, and the mathematical sciences, and the experimental questionings and daring onslaught of infidelity, and the interesting domain of purely Christian authorship, there is as much as, it might be supposed, would enforce intense application in every direction. It might be supposed that all truth was not so evidently unfolded as to excuse the cessation of research and scrutiny; or if so, it might be surmised that the ponderous volumes, and the no less ponderous thinking, of Owen, Barrow, Baxter, Taylor, Hooker, Augustine, Origen, or Calvin, might be worthy of some attention, and that, in dealing out immortal bread to the lost and perishing, some argument might be furnished or powerful incentive supplied by these minds which might be available in the conversion of creatures to their Creator, and might make more patent the path by which a return was rendered possible. Dead, indeed, must be that soul to the cause of worthy ambition—callous his nature—who can afford to be insensible to the grandeur of those works which are scattered around him in such profusion, or to the suggestions they are the means of making, or the sciences which have grown out of them, or the imagery taken from them, in which man has embodied the domain of thought, rendering palpable the spiritual by the physical—commencing with matter, and evolving from its cold obstruction those grand truths which lead him to the knowledge of an all-powerful and all-pervading Mind.

Between the study of Nature and that of Revelation there is no such disagreement as is supposed: both of them are allowed to proceed from the same great Author. Revelation has its domain, and so has science. Nor do we think that any ministerial duty is violated, though the whole habit of a minister's mind led him to studies of a kindred character with those to which one of the most efficient ministers of modern days applied the powers of his exalted intellect, when he composed the following beautiful observations:—"Instead of the temple of science having been reared, it were more proper to say that the temple of Nature had been evolved. The archetype of science is the universe; and it is in the disclosure of its successive parts that science advances from step to step, not properly raising any new architecture of its own, but rather unveiling, by degrees, an architecture as old as creation. The labourers in philosophy create nothing, but only bring out into exhibition that which was before created. And there is a resulting harmony in their labours, however widely apart from each other they have been prosecuted, not because they have adjusted one part to another, but because the adjustment has been already made to their hands. There comes forth, it is true, of their labours a most magnificent harmony, yet not a harmony which they have made, but a pre-existent harmony which they have only made visible."

We could not regard ourselves as having yet done our duty to this part of our subject without referring to that which, if ministers do not themselves, some censure may be inflicted on them by a public, perhaps too glad to find "an occasion against them." "If we judge ourselves we should not be judged." I allude to self-discipline and charity. A minister may attain a a large share of public respect, if his general conduct is such as the world is fitted to appreciate. He may not have been called to show any very eminent qualities—any high trait of generosity, or disinterestedness, or self-denial, or sympathy with the destitute, or making himself an almoner to them, or affording that visible assistance which they are in need of. He is not usually expected to do so. Indeed his income, when compared to the demands of his station, is hardly sufficient to allow a scale of charity very profuse or frequent. But it were a bad and reprehensible habit of thought, did he entertain the idea that the deed of charity was one of those secular duties, out of the sphere in which he moved, or that though very obligatory on the community, he, by his position, was released from the duty of liberality. There is nothing in the clerical character which forbids him to alleviate the sufferings of the wretched; to wipe the tear of misery away;

to "deliver the poor that cried, and the fatherless, and him that had none to help him, so that the blessing of him that was ready to perish might come upon him; or to cause the widow's heart to sing for joy; or to put on righteousness, so that it might clothe him; or to become eyes to the blind, or feet to the lame; or to search out the cause which he knew not; or to break the jaws of the wicked, and pluck the spoil out their teeth." Nor do we know that a minister's dignity would suffer, though what was said of Levett, by Johnson, were said of him—

> "In misery's darkest caverns known,
> His ready aid was ever nigh,
> Where hopeless anguish poured his groan,
> And lonely want retired to die."

Whatever may be said, to be the minister of afflicted humanity; to raise the fallen; to restore the offending; to reclaim the outcast; these, the best declaration of the Gospel message, shall be the delight of the true minister now, and his crown and rejoicing "when the righteous Judge appears."

There is a certain class of the community so woefully fallen, so apparently despised or neglected, that they cannot believe that the world, which has abandoned them to misery or indigence, would be at the pains to make any organization to bring them back again. The anguish of their ruminations compels them to unbelief. They stand off in sullen disregard of any operation for their welfare. The very belief in an Almighty Caretaker has perhaps given way. They cannot believe that the Being who seems to have abandoned them to so severe affliction cares for them to that degree spoken of in the Gospel. Now, the only way to find access to hearts hardened to an unearthly obduracy is by kindness, and, if possible, by material aid and by display of a common humanity. The exhibition of any superiority in imparting spiritual advice is not what they need, or, whether they need it or not, is not what they will receive. To know that a salary is attached to a visitor is, for the time, the destruction of his mission in their eyes. It becomes him, therefore, who would do good here, to show that his object is to put to flight all misery; to redress, if possible, every grievance, and minister judiciously of the little substance which pertains to him where it is required.

Prayer and preaching are not to be considered mechanical performances, regulated by line and measure, and having no *rationale* in the nature of things; not some doings of a particular craft, and belonging to craftsmen who exercise it. It is the duty of every man to exhort his neighbour "for his good to edifying," and to ask for him the descent of influences supernal and divine. But it has been thought right and advisable, by the Author of Christianity, that there should be a class who might, free from distraction, give themselves "perpetually to the ministry of the word and to prayer," not as though they were to be the only traffickers in these "goodly pearls," or were to form a kind of monopoly, but only to deal out, in the most judicious manner and largest measure, a commodity which required attention and time. And these purely ministerial and regulated duties do not belong to him in such a way as to exclude him from those fine features of character which prove him, by sympathy, affection, and liberality, to be a human being.

Perhaps it may be affirmed of ministerial functionaries, that it must be from the privacy of their closet that they may tell most effectually on the outside world, without trying to have an actual bearing on great questions, or too much seeking the glare of public observation. The closet must be the scene of their noblest labours and most pious meditations: and there was a time when, with little demand made en them by the common and every-day world, and when left to their own solitary meditations, they laboured and finished the finest trophies of their knowledge and their zeal. It might be concluded that ministers lose not a little of their dignity by standing too much in the gaze of the world. Their place is not to be absorbed into worldly society or parties, but rather to stand in the distance, and come upon the world with some preparation worthy of audience. Their place is to be in the world, but not of it; not to affect peculiarity of language or custom, but keep before others, in their walk and manners, the truths they assert and the doctrines they maintain. The moment a people could say, "He is one of ourselves; not distinct in life, not superior in learning or talent," we suppose his value was depreciated as a gospel minister.

"Ye are not of the world; I have chosen ye out of the world; were ye of the world, the world would love his own." We may infer from these words, which we apprehend are as true now as when first audibly pronounced, that, without an affectation of singularity or manners of an anchorite, ministers dwell on one side, and the world has its stand on the other; and that their mixing with the world ought to resemble rather the excursion of a temporary and occasional assailant than a permanent and satisfied inhabitant. It follows plainly from this, if the sacred herald of the cross be not rendered distinct in any one way from the external world, he has become one of themselves, and with the garb, it may be, of a minister, has no distinction but in apparel. To exert his purest influences on the world, it is necessary that it deem him one vested with a real embassy, coming to them with a beneficent and holy commission, an envoy sent from a superior court, a delegate deputed from one higher than a terrestrial monarch, one armed with all the array of credentials, bearing on them the stamp and commission of the seal of Heaven.

It cannot give a high view of the grandeur of the office if it be found allied to secular managements, or constantly insisting on temporalities; or, unmindful of the provision which is promised, it manifest a cleaving to the sensible and secular. We cannot fancy that such expressions as, "the labourer is worthy of his hire," and "the officiator at the altar should eat of its offerings," were intended to impart a habit of thought quite secular, or produce cupidity, or envy of greater opulence or greater comfort. Injury perhaps is done; usefulness is impaired, if it be once insinuated that the workman in the vineyard of the Messiah makes the same selfish contract which an ordinary labourer makes with his employer. The spiritual workman's reward is supposed to be his Master's approval and a celestial crown. It is not a system of terrestrial negotiation. The forms of the merchantman are here to be abjured. The trafficking of earthly business is here out of place. The intense avidity for gain, excusable in the world, is here to be repudiated. With abundant respect to the plea that the ministers of the altar must have a provision, in some degree commensurate to their demands; yet, as sent by Christ Himself, their reward must, in a great measure, come from Him. It is not the world which employs them. It is one greater than the world. And though earth, with all its decorations, dignity, and luxury, were at their bidding, yet their essential recompense must be from Him who seeth their secret labours and prayers, and will openly reward them.

Meanwhile, it may be accepted as an indication how much the community have begun to appreciate a zealous and working ministry, in that their liberality in the cause has greatly increased. This, we think, is a real intimation also what estimate they put on the great Teacher of Christianity. The amount of their liberality increased, is the amount of their avidity for wealth or of their excessive expenditure diminished. If they esteem the vast benefits conferred at their proper value, they cannot do too much to put these spiritual workmen on a footing of proper efficiency. We do not certainly hear now of those harrowing details which were at one time common enough, when the necessities of a limited condition, we are afraid, sadly reduced their usefulness; when the urgent claims of the hour, and frequently distressing embarrassments, filled their souls with gloomy apprehensions for the future, interrupted the tranquillity of the study, and forbade all approaches to a class of society in the least removed out of their sphere.*

With all the anxiety about an earthly competency done away, we should naturally anticipate greater efforts at preparation, more laboured and finished produce, more devotedness and philanthropy. All this is, we think, on the increase. Talent is better cultivated. With the increase of books has come the necessity for more literary exertion. A reading and discriminating public will exalt the whole area of society, and raise the ministerial body to the position they were intended to occupy. In some instances literature is actually becoming flimsy; in others is becoming irreverent, diverging from the soberness of true philosophy, and deeming that from some petty and equivocal specimen or discovery it may cast an aspersion

---

* A great improvement in this respect has taken place, but not in proportion to the increase of wealth and comfort among the people.

on a whole system. In these circumstances, it becomes the guardians of the people's creed to exert the best of their powers to meet assailants on their own ground. And this can only be "by pureness, by knowledge"; by bringing the whole life and conduct into keeping with the Gospel model; by moral features of character which all can appreciate; and by achievements on the field of literature, by which they may even surpass, in their own department, and foil, with their own weapons, the impugners of their creed and assailants of the humble piety and faith of their forefathers.

CHAPTER IX.

WE shall now make a few concluding observations intended to have an equal bearing on most of the subjects which, in this treatise, have been already alluded to. An encouragement has been given, and been readily accepted, because it saves from the necessity of labour and examination, to believe that the religion of Jesus is a scheme so simple and obvious, so legible in its grand contour, and so limited in its propositions, that the most unsophisticated and unlettered mind may read in it the impress of the Divinity, and be convinced by an array of evidence altogether irresistible. Thus, how often is it affirmed that "the wisdom of the world is foolishness with God;" that He "makes wise the simple;" that "out of the mouth of babes and sucklings He has perfected praise?" And these words have been usually thought to refer to the ease wherewith Christianity is understood; wherewith this grand system is comprehended; the clearness and legibility wherewith its great objects lie revealed in all their patency before the eye of the understanding, as if it were some territory the eye was directed to, and which, shining in the splendour of unclouded sunshine, presented all its contents and all its objects invested in the brilliancy which fell upon itself.

Now, what we would enquire here is, does this representation agree with the statements of the divine word itself, that Christianity is like some gross material, which to inspect we have only to allow our gaze to wander over the scene or the object before us? Was this the way the prophets and martyrs of ancient times received the knowledge of "Christ, and of Him crucified"? If it be true that the words may flash upon the mind, yet is it not true that the substance must accompany the words and be appropriated by the mind? It is a fact that, in a month's time, it is quite possible to have accomplished the task of knowing all that lies contained in the Revelation of God, from the first chapter of Genesis to the last of the Apocalypse. But does that hurried perusal of the contents imply the pondering, the contemplation, the reception on the soul of all the grand objects and influences contained therein? Might that task not be performed without the individual being made a Christian at all? Will the mind, in a scanning so hasty, be able to take in all the grandeur, the sublimity, which a communication from the Supreme may be supposed to possess? Will it be imbued with a new spirit? Will a new sentiment be imparted from a hurried march over this sacred territory?

Different views may be taken of the whole matter. Our view of it is, perhaps, not frequently submitted or dwelt upon ; and yet what cannot but be suggested to the reflecting mind is the one we shall now advert to. It is altogether reasonable to suppose that, *à priori*, we may pronounce the person best fitted to understand Christianity, to venerate such an economy of benevolence to the unworthy, would be the man who himself delighted in the act of benevolence and could, therefore, estimate the benevolent doings of another. From the natural we ascend to the spiritual. The virtuoso, who at once recognizes the stamp and lineaments of one of the great masters on the canvas, is not the factitious or professional connoisseur, but is the man whose nature is touched by something to which he cannot give expression and cannot explain. There is a spirit within him naturally affected by an adequate object. He can see the mighty intellect of the painter beaming from his workmanship. He discerns it in some line or feature; and if we suppose that by some wonderful disaster which obliterated the authors' names, but left their performances, their names had passed into oblivion, yet the productions of the Raphaels, Corregios, da Vincis, Angelos, Titians, Turners would, though their names were lost, impress this genial spectator in such a way that he would award to them the praise of superior excellency, and they, in the light of their own evidence, would probably occupy before the world a position as eminent and conspicuous as they at present possess.

May it not, after all, be the man of expansive nature and lofty aspirations, with heart filled with benevolence, who is fitted to appreciate the loveliness of Christianity? Is there any irrev-

erence in the supposition; for we have not said that this love of
the excellent and the good and beautiful—that this moral
discrimination—is conversion? We only suppose that there is,
in such a nature, something that, at least, brings him by an
innate impulse into contact with the Gospel narrative. And we
might say that even the man whose conceptions are brilliant
and numerous—whose imagination exposes its sensitive tablet to
the influences which flow from the beautiful or majestic in
natural scenery, and whose disposition naturally demands its
congenial satisfaction in the task of perusing or knowing the
thoughts of other minds—this man is in a much more likely
position for becoming a Christian than one whose mind seldom
or never rises beyond his diurnal drudgery, or the indispensable
provision which supports him. The enquiring and examining
disposition—the mind which delights to trace up the stream of
time, and survey the empires and states, the broken glories of
which line its banks—the soul that can be affected by the spectacle
of what is grand and what is benevolent—who would not say
that this quality of mind was more favourable to the proper
appreciation of Christianity than the opposite? Has the touching
narrative of some magnificent doing of self-denial on earth no
affinity to the act of self-denial in heaven, when we are told that
"God so loved the world as to give His Son"? Which of the
two would likely be more affected at reading this astonishing
verse, that "God so loved the world as to give His Son, that
whosoever believeth on Him should not perish"? Would it be
the man whose soul was cast into a tumult of agitation by reading the story of an earthly monarch sending his son among the
inhabitants of a revolted province, in order to convey to them
the tidings of his father's goodwill, or would it be he whose
impassive nature was wholly unmoved by the touching episode?
Is there any difference in the exhibition, more than arises from
locality and person? A man's giving up his son to die for the
rebellious—this is one term. God's giving up His Son to die
for the rebellious—this is the other term. The act seems to be
the same. The principle of unsubdued affection is the same.
It is God who is the agent in the one case. It is man in the
other.

This renders it plain that a world of benevolent and high-minded beings would give a more favourable reception to Christianity than would a world of the opposite character. There might be peculiar qualities of mind that may impel the one to ply the labour of diligent search and incessant meditation; and if a man from all this labour come out a Christian, we should naturally suppose him to be a better Christian than another who never troubled himself with the matter. This, it is true, might land us in the conclusion that it is impossible for some to be Christians at all, as the appreciative quality is lacking in a great degree to them. But let it be observed, that we are reasoning of what likely would take place, and not of conversion; for due appreciation of the venerable, and the worthy, and the excellent in Christianity may, without certain other requirements, be no more conversion than the recognition which the mind takes of the beautiful and grand in art or nature is conversion.

By conversion we certainly must mean something in the form of a change which is wrought among the tendencies and faculties of the soul. And the question would come to be, as there may be some with souls fitted to admire the grandeur and goodwill exhibited in the Christian system, may there not be some whom the Holy Spirit might delight to assist with His presence and influences more than others? Might there not be some in whose souls He would be more at home than others? The question comes to be, might not a favourably organized nature present that very opening through which His entrance, to irradiate and to bless, might be made? We are not at all sure of this. But of this we are certain, that the man whose life is surrounded with the halo of virtue, whose heart dilates with the impulse of generosity, would present a more impressive exhibition as a Christian than the person whose heart could be affected by no appeal, however urgent; even on the supposition both were converted. The man who "deviseth liberal things," and he who feels as if the least participation with his brother were a loss of something to himself, might still, after conversion, be distinguished by peculiar characteristics, and might, by those who did not know their character, be styled by the peculiar epithet which belonged to them. We do not, however, suppose-that, from any ruling quality, the covetous man or the voluptuary is beyond the reach of those sovereign influences which may extend to all. Yet the one somehow impresses us as having something in him on which the Spirit may more readily operate. The other character causes us to entertain a different impression.

But the admiration of a doctrine is different from being the subject of the influences which the doctrine implies. It is possible to be elevated to transport by reading the words that "God gave His Son," without believing in that Son. The grandeur of the Donor, the benevolence which impelled Him to this rare and costly sacrifice, and the inestimable preciousness of the gift, are fitted to act on the highest qualities of the natural man, without making him a believer. If he has imagination, it will be exercised to its highest reach in figuring the Supreme and Eternal actually sending His Son on the errand of mercy. If he has benevolence, it will sympathise with the mighty benefaction. By the recoil which he would be most sensitively alive to if asked, for some great cause of philanthropy, to give his own son, he may contemplate the ardency of that affection which dwelt in the bosom of "the King Eternal."

Some natures may not be so able to sympathise with those sublime doings, yet they are not beyond the reach of that grace which may impress their souls. But certainly we have no reason for saying that Christianity is so easily understood, if by this we mean that thoughtlessness may understand it; that earthliness may understand it; that indifference may understand it. It may imply such forth-putting of the faculties as that the man who makes a strenuous effort may alone understand it. Thus, " the wise shall understand." The Newtonian would not be so designated unless he comprehended the principles, and perhaps breathed the spirit of Newton. The Baconian could never claim the proud honour of such a discipleship did he not know in what distinct characteristic it was that Bacon became the foremost man among the philosophers, and opened the true path to the investigation of Nature's mysteries. But while, without labour and attention, no one can attain to these terrestrial distinctions, it is too frequently imagined that, without labour or endeavour, any one may become a Christian. This has arisen from a judgment concerning conversion, that it is some capricious and arbitrary operation which, in a single moment, may take place on the human soul, so that a man might be said to be one moment the most worthless character, and the next might outstrip all competition in grandeur and dignity, and be invested with a title to a mansion and honours which will never fade or decay.

The sacred teacher who expounds "the lively oracles," requires to be on his guard about pronouncing on a matter so mysterious. A change may be said to have occurred when it has not occurred. We object to the hasty generalization which makes one case a rule for all, because it may render null and void the grand principles of eternal morality. Perhaps where conversion is genuine, it is not the hasty process it is declared to be, as we know not through what stages of developing light and knowledge the believer may have been carried on the career of virtue and piety on which he has entered.

It were a pernicious endeavour to try and produce an impression, as if, in conversion, the laws of virtue were repealed by a court superior to virtue. It were a miserable business to represent Christianity, and high principle, and moral rectitude as at variance. It were nearly the same as saying to any particular individual, "The law of gravitation is suspended in your favour; you may let yourself go from your giddy elevation without fear." Christianity and morality are not incompatible. The true Christian will display the grandest morality. And yet the divine system is sometimes exhibited as if high principle and rigid morality detracted from the Christian, as if by them he lost his true and substantial honours. There is a tacit agreement among Christians to make little of the virtues of rectitude, fidelity, and unswerving truthfulness, just as there is among moralists to build on these virtues and ignore Christianity. One side forgets the insufficiency of human virtue in its noblest exhibitions to give admittance to the bowers of immortality. And both sides forget its sufficiency to show that there may be a willingness and endeavour to render obedience to the divine statutes which have been enacted.

It would be an advantage if the essentials of the Gospel

system were vindicated without losing sight of the indispensable necessity for the virtues of justice, righteousness, and truth. There may be a danger of a Gospel which enjoins no duty, and removes every burden, being misunderstood. There may be the danger of making the pathway so easy that the utterance of a few cabala may be allowed to carry, without labour or effort, to the height of blessedness. The pulpit may hold forth the "form of sound words" so that the ears of an audience are delighted with the sound, and too often think that the utterance of a verse may charm their advancement to life everlasting. Infidelity has had too much reason for saying, that there seems to be an antipathy between the Christian religion and morality; but this is only with some of its vindicators, some of its inconsiderate friends. The Gospel itself inculcates the grandest morality.

Thus the press, in the path of reform, is considered an advance on the pulpit. The press is, no doubt, a most powerful organ for the removal of grievances, and remedying the moral disorders of the community, and for vindicating liberty of thought, having one advantage in this respect, that the field of its opera-tions is so wide, and its subjects so numerous and interesting. It is permitted to exercise a censorship regarding subjects the mention of which would be held to be degrading to the pulpit. A sacred halo surrounds the latter, and its functions cannot descend to what is earthly and secular. A particular and set phraseology has been its natural and uniform language—so uniform, indeed, that a departure from it would become notice-able and unbecoming. A discourse on political economy, or revolutions, or parties, would be a surrender of its dignity. To investigate the principles of natural philosophy would be a desecration of the honour which belongs to it. The sublimest walk in astronomy, or an explanation of that optical instrument by which some of its conjectures have been changed into certain-ties, would be at once acknowledged as out of place. The themes which may grace a social science congress cannot grace the pulpit. There is a felt wrong done to the day if such themes be entertained.

This is not because there is anything in the pulpit adverse to the progress of science, but because its domain is wholly different from that of the philosopher. Each has his own domain, and each may grace and dignify his own territory. Each may expatiate aright and satisfactorily on the subject which falls within his province. The pulpit cannot suffer disparagement because it is not the press, more than the press must suffer detriment because it is not the pulpit. The business of the social system is the work of the press—its becoming employment. The conversion of man, as a candidate for heaven, is the work of the pulpit—its befitting occupation. Were the minister to enter on the territory consigned to the press, he would be going out of his own. Were the press to assume the discussion of purely theological doctrines, it would be leaving its own department—neglecting a labour which cannot be done by the other. It is well that each has its region assigned to it. Each may be the channel of usefulness; while they must be diminished in their efficiency if they cross the frontiers which mark and bound each other's dominions.

And yet the pulpit is charged with neglect or indifference because it does not assume powers that do not belong to it. It is for it to enforce, by the most powerful arguments it can devise, the lessons of piety, and patience, and resignation, and the necessity for an atoning sacrifice and mediatorial intercession; and if it succeed in doing so, shall it be said that it is a dispensable instrument; that its disclosures are unnecessary; that society could do without it; that it is inferior to, and far behind the achievements and advancement of, a secular press and secular literature? And how can any one say what precise good the pulpit may accomplish? For aught we know to the contrary, whatever is virtuous and noble in literature may emanate from its explanations. For aught we know, the cause of philanthropy may have flourished best in the hands of the men who were trained at its foot. For aught we know, civilization may have had a vast impulse added to it from the lessons dealt out in the sanctuary. Though it afforded the means of a mere surface dressing; though it had not attained the efficiency of which it is capable; though it were chargeable with dogmatism in its doctrines and want of fervour in its persuasions, yet we cannot conceive of such an agency operating on such immense multitudes without powerfully promoting civil order in the state, domestic concord in families, and the cause of knowledge far more than that of ignorance.

What goes to confirm our position is, that the worst portion of the community are those who never come near its lessons; who look with suspicion on its efforts, or with envy on its dignitaries. Even though it fell far short of the high reach of successful philanthropy which it might attain, yet such is the rebuke given to vice, infamy, and degradation by its mere existence; such is the silent reproach it casts upon iniquity, that the existence of a single centre from which light and the holy lessons of celestial wisdom are wont to emanate over the community, is such that all "iniquity, as ashamed, hides its face," or betakes itself to a quarter where it may best perpetrate its nefarious designs. It is a deterrent from sin. And such is its secret influence, that if the experiment were tried of doing without its sabbatical labours, certain we are that it would be an experiment fatal to the grandest interests of humanity. Its removal would be the signal to the leaders in iniquity to muster their forces, and ply all their energies, and let loose the horrors of an anarchy and confusion on a community no longer restrained by the sense of a Superior Power— with all the rancorous malevolence and pernicious passions of nature allowed to revel in the commission of every enormity. As for a Christian Sabbath, it would be at once brought down from the sacredness which now marks it. With the desuetude of its decency, and its particular dress, and its exercises, would depart the day itself, no longer distinguished by any peculiar badge from the other days of the week.

We could not indeed measure the amount of the disaster, or the injury inflicted on the cause of civilization. The removal of this instrument would be the removal of everything associated with it; not only of the solemnities of the one day in the seven; not only of the order who occupy it, but of the very system whose lessons and doctrines it is intended to unfold. And perhaps a "dearth of the word of God" might be found to be attended with more inconvenience than could be remedied by all the expedients in the power of the political economist to suggest. It is true armies might be enlisted and paraded, and, with the celerity of science, might be marched on the scene of disaffection and havoc. The word might be given with magisterial authority for that discharge which would carry death among the inhabitants. The leaders in the van of insubordination might be seized upon by the talons of justice, and be duly tried, convicted, and punished. But where would be that agency by which the peaceful and orderly throng wont to pass, with hearts to some extent distended with the element of genial charity and resignation, to the abode of prayer? Where would be those compositions of piety, during the hearing of which every effervescence of unholy passion had a quietus laid upon its unsanctified workings, and, thereby, the time of its ungoverned outbreaking retarded, if not wholly prevented? Where would be those prayers which, listened to with the listlessness of utter indifference, still must leave such an effect behind them as would be a kind of counteraction to the turbulance of appetite, to the suggestions or doings of sin? Where would be those melodious outbreathings fitted, in some degree, to impress the most obdurate, and remind the pious of the choirs and the anthems of the Zion which is above? And where, we ask, would be the effect which is produced on the history and habits of every attendant in the house of prayer? Where would be those energies which used to find an outlet for their activity? Turned, perhaps, to the carnage of civil discord, the new arrangements of spoliation, or the phrensy of revolutionary violence, these energies, undirected by religious principle, and left to produce their natural results, would spread horror and extermination over a land in which every principle of piety and obedience, earthly and heavenly, was demolished by the demolition of the abodes of piety and peace, where these sentiments were inculcated.

It must be observed that there is a class in society naturally pacific in their dispositions, and whose wish is to pass their days in tranquillity. Perhaps, with all to lose and nothing to gain by the uproar of disorder, they may see it to be their interest that the customary state of matters be maintained. They have no desire for a change, because to them a change would be from better to worse. They are sure they would not advance but retrograde under another arrangement from what is. But how would it be with them who had all to gain and nothing to lose, which constitute a large portion of every community? Do we suppose that the disregard paid to the authority of Heaven, implied by the disregard paid to its house on earth, would have the effect of a tranquillizing process? And when we are reminded of the gross and unapprehensive ignorance in which a portion of society exist; that the little virtue which they possess arises greatly from veneration for some cherished name or from the view of what they cannot understand, but are still disposed to idolize, could we venture to expect a beneficial result if, expecting all the hardihood of matured virtue, all the resistance to temptation such virtue would present, we at once abolished all the incentives to devotion, or piety, or loyalty, under the guise of the extermination of superstition and idolatry?

But though the pulpit possessed more a negative than a positive effect on the community, it would be downright madness to make any attempt at its suppression. When an institution, of whatever kind, has entwined itself with the most hallowed associations, to endanger the existence of that institution would be a most hazardous adventure on the part of politicians. It would be putting in peril their best interests and civil security. Yet many suppose that the time is coming when, from the refinements and extent of legislation, people, by the mere force of proper enactments in the earthly statute-book, will be retained in becoming subjection to superiors, and endowed with sentiments of respect to established forms and usages. But there is a mistake here with regard to what law can do. It can only go a certain length. But it is incompetent to implant a new sentiment, such as respect for the property procured by another's toil and exertion, or respect for person and life. This is not the part of law at all. It is its part to deter from crime by holding out the penalty, by announcing the punishment which will be inflicted. If the criminal thinks that he may either, by the number of the disobedient, become too powerful for the law, or evade its penalty by his cunning, then it is evident that the law has done all it can do. It plainly derives its power from the number of those who render compliance to its enactments. But should an equal number rise in insurrection against them, it becomes feeble and inoperative.

In such a state of matters, of how much consequence it is for the law to possess a powerful ally, which may endeavour to impart a new principle; to produce an equilibrium between the nobler powers of the soul and the tumultuous agitations which sometimes gain the ascendency and suppress its higher longings. Law cannot invest with either the power or principle of obedience. It is powerless to do this. It may hold out its forbidding terrors. It may raise the interdictory partition on the other side of which the infatuated child of rebellion may meet with the punishment due to his crimes. It may connect safety and security with obedience, and punishment with disobedience.· And should another agency present itself, which may convey or cherish the principle of loyalty, then how much should this auxiliary power—this new reinforcement—be welcomed by the law-maker, and every obstruction in the way of the proper action of this new co-operation be taken out of the way? It is the business of the political economist to devise the most effectual means to give free scope to both instruments; to the law, that it may maintain the well-doer in all his civil immunities and restrain the evil-doer by proper coercions; to the ministry of the Word, that they may strengthen, if possible, the principle of obedience and of respect to all vested with authority.

Independent of the evidences by which Christianity is accredited to the minds of the intellectual, and of the doctrines which it teaches, there is something in the persuasives to order and resignation which it presents that is fitted to make good citizens. Independent of the ennobling anticipation which it inspires, and the boundless prospect it unfolds, there is something in it by which it renders man more fitted to associate with his fellow-man. It cultivates gratitude, and evokes a spirit of forgiveness. It suppresses the strong feeling of resentment. It presents this life as something extremely insignificant when we look at the immensity of eternity. Supported by the light reflected from the future glory, man may be less careful about the present allotment, the present profit, the present suffering. With considerations like these, he will not regard this world as the only one with which he will ever be connected; and, in the peerless value of objects indestructible and permanent, he will learn to attach less importance to those which are fleeting and temporary. To obtain them, he will not oppose any principle of scrupulous honesty. If he lose them by the artifices of fraud, he will not follow the spoiler with the determined purposes of vengeance. If he has suffered wrong, if the foe has been unpitying, he will rather try to "heap coals of fire" on the perpetrator's head than imitate his example, and do wrong in return. Should his character be aspersed, or his good name be tarnished with the breath of calumny; should envy blacken the virtues and ennobling principles which it cannot attain, his truly Christian weapons are forgiveness and prayer—forgiveness to the wrong-doer, and prayer for his amendment and salvation.

Surely such a discipline as this has sufficient merit connected with it, and has so many of the honours of its past services to display, to recommend it to the statesman as the only system which, if maintained in its active influences, may spread around the land the graces of due respect for all authority, and obedience to those edicts which the wisdom of the nation may enjoin. There is no way of making man a more obedient and orderly citizen than the way of making him a good Christian. If he be the latter, his circumstances will make no difference—he will surely be the former. Let his destitution be as severe and trying as it may, he will consider it an infliction from Heaven, and will not betake himself to the artifices of the peculator, or dealer in games of chance, or services of infamy, in order to procure that competency which is denied him for a moment. Let the cloud which overcasts his prospects be as black as it may, he will not add to it the desecration of his own conscientious principles. He will sustain, in their integrity, those principles which may have come down to him the birthright of a hundred generations. And dearer to his soul will be their unsullied purity than all the substance of the opulent, than all the vanity of the proud.

There is evidently something in Christianity fitted to preserve it as with a healthful salt, and fitted to perpetuate it to far distant generations. Its evidences, though oft assailed, have received on their front many a mark of the adversary's onset, and yet remain in all their integrity. Its fortress has withstood all the rampant efforts of infidelity. Their mightiest champions have assailed it, and it still remains. The flippancy of Voltaire; the subtlety and intellect of Hume, the most gigantic and penetrating of its adversaries; the vulgarity of Paine; the superseding, dreamy, and mystic inventiveness of Renan, the most interesting of its foes, have all been met and successfully resisted. It is true that Christianity, like any other system, depends on human attachments, human views, human intellect; and we think there is something in the dispensation revealed in the New Testament fitted to win the respect of every honest enquirer; and of intellect, where it is associated with high moral emotions and the candour of the sincere investigator.

Were this system chargeable with anything like imposition, it is tantamount to charging its disciples with idolatry. Indeed, we know not how its adherents could be freed from this grave charge if Christianity were untrue. It is impossible for beings whose view is limited on all sides to pronounce conclusively on many grand and important questions which seem to affect their destiny and to give a complexion to their eternity. But we know of nothing that can either supersede the present economy or render Christianity, with all its inducements, arguments, and virtues, less necessary. There is an apparent adaptation in it to the felt wants and yearnings of the human soul. It may satisfy longing desires for the infinite, and a restless inquisitiveness about the reason of the present condition, and the certainty of the future prospect. It comes in as the complement of Natural Theology. If the one reasons and concludes that I have a soul, the other gladdens me with the information that it is redeemed. If the one tells me of an eternity in which I have to expatiate, the other tells me of its character and blessedness.

Besides, there is nothing in a communication from Heaven which renders it unlikely. Every event, when considered *à priori*, is unlikely. Prior to their occurrence, there are millions of chances against any combination of events taking place. It is unlikely, *à priori*, that the sun is inhabited. It is unlikely that this globe will change its axis of revolution. It is very unlikely that the sea should want its tide at the proper period. It is unlikely that any supposed coincidence should occur; but after the event the unlikelihood disappears. Because there is not a constant intercourse sustained with this world now, and visible messengers have ceased to shed a glory over its plains or villages, we would derive the unlikelihood that they have ever done so. Were they, in direct manifestation, and before a proper array of witnesses, now to do so; were the earth to be visited as we are informed it was of old; were angelic squadrons to descend on this orb; were miracles now to dazzle the eyes of the multitude, there would be no unlikelihood. Taking place makes anything vraisemblable. Experience is the only guide. If these events would cease to be improbable the moment they occur, why should they be deemed unlikely if they are affirmed, on sufficient evidence, to have occurred? The fact is stript of its improbability by being a fact. Should it not be stript of it, by being attested by credible witnesses as having occurred? Can history only accredit events within the compass of every-day experience? Then history cannot accredit miracles; then a miracle cannot be accredited as having taken place. Then there is something which has taken place, but cannot be delivered on the page of history to succeeding generations. Then a Revelation can be no more accredited, for it is a miracle requiring after-miracles for its attestation. It would in this way be impossible to inform a future age of a miraculous dispensation, however desirable to effect the object of that dispensation.

We know not how it is possible to assert that Christianity cannot be accredited with evidence of miracles, and why the supernatural tidings may not come down, in all the irradiation of a light from the sanctuary above, to the present generation. Do they who would cast an imputation on the facts of Christianity, profess to have been present when these facts were said to have taken place? Did they witness any of the ordinary doings of Christ's history? Yet they would by no means deny these ordinary events, nor that He wrought at the trade of His reputed father, nor that He went up to the Passover, nor that He acquired celebrity as a great teacher; and this because they are common, come within the limits of their own experience. But they deny the others, as giving sight to the blind, or curing

I

the diseased, or raising the dead, because they go beyond the circle of their experience. In other words, they make their experience the reason for withholding their belief from the facts of Christianity. But would they make this same experience any longer a defence for their unbelief if the events really took place before their eyes; if they were spectators on the spot? But the events are narrated to us by those who were spectators on the spot. They had experience of them. They testified what they really saw. It would appear then as if, in the case of a miracle, they would only believe their own experience, but not that of any number of witnesses, however honest; of any attestations, however imposing and solemn.

Now, the circumstances of the case forbid us to have any experience on this matter; and yet it is a matter which most materially affects our highest interests. If we enquire, we shall find. If we ask, it shall be given us. If we knock, "it shall be opened unto us." These are the grand moral preliminaries towards our effectual understanding of Revelation, towards the opening up of its mysteries, towards their manifestation to the understanding. In this case, no sincere investigator shall be doomed to disappointment. Infidelity, elevated with its generalities and its theories, is frequently destined to lose its way in the clouds and darkness it has raised. Looking at one side of the matter, but seldom venturing on the adverse arguments of its opponents, it cannot be expected to decide the case before its tribunal with impartiality. And how can it ever attain to any rigorous conclusion on the whole question, or pronounce decisively on doings which may bear a relation to immensity of space or eternity of duration? The pride of intellect, with its arguments and enchantments, causes them to affirm previously to any decided proofs or powerful evidence they may have attained. It is the precipitate temerity of intellect so to affirm, even before they have gained the evidence which their investigations might have afterwards afforded.

Christianity we believe yet to be in the vigour of a fadeless prime. It never grows old. If anything at all, Christianity, as formed to meet the case of fallen man, must remain. It is based on facts. Its doctrines are not the dreams of visionaries.

To it belongs the stable foundation of events testified and evidenced by many witnesses. Link by link, in close connection, has it come down to the present day. If ministers be true to the employment of those grand instrumentalities; if they mingle their teaching with those gracious and impressive displays of kindliness and fine lineaments of character, such as the unchristian may estimate, with the spread of the Gospel, power will be given to it. It would be well, indeed, and worth thousands of treatises, if enforced by the power of a praiseworthy conversation the infidel would say—"No philosophy, no system, could produce such deportment as this; I will be a Christian too." We are afraid doctrine and conduct sometimes suffer a separation, and Christians endeavour rather to derive their complacency from the doctrines they profess than from the conduct these doctrines should produce.

Every one may not attain to the realization of the grand sentiment from Channing, in which a great deal of what has been expanded in this treatise may find itself briefly and strikingly expressed—"Eloquence is not a trick of words; it is the utterance of great truths so clearly discerned, so deeply felt, so bright, so burning, that they cannot be confined; that they create for themselves style and manner which carry them far into other souls; and of this eloquence there is but one fount, and that is inward life, force of thought, force of feeling." Every one can exhibit, however, the most valuable and impressive exhibitions of rectitude in conduct, of benevolence in action, and of self-denial in life. And this will be, at least, as effectual, when displayed in conjunction with the ennobling principles and emotions which give rise to it, as the eloquence of a Massillon, a Bossuet, or a Chalmers.

All the evidences of Christianity may be repelled by the bold and defiant defenders of infidelity. They are prepared to meet them. To attack them thus, is to attack a fortress without proper artillery. But they would neither be ashamed nor afraid to yield, did Christians show such a connection between their system and conversation as to declare it a superior system, by its fitness to lead to superior conduct. It might thus be in the power of a Christian community to convert the world, as it is in their power by an opposite deportment to disparage the grandeur and loveliness of Christianity. The strongest evidences of Christianity plainly lie in the virtues of Christians themselves. Without these virtues, a man would be a Christian in name, and not a Christian indeed.

Ministers may make their most strenuous endeavours, and may find a resistance at the human heart not so easy to surmount. Old Adam, in the stronghold of his entrenchments, and armed with his delusions, may be too strong for young Melancthon. But what, by their varied endowments and appliances, they cannot do themselves, there is One, to whom at all times they may have recourse, who can do it for them. Christianity acknowledges this as their most powerful auxiliary in the work in which they are engaged. Let them never despair while the gracious throne is accessible, and the way which leads to it has every obstruction removed. Let them know that prayer, and faith, and effort are destined to level, at last, the mountains of difficulty which lie in their way. Let them bring forth their armour, in the shape of scholarship, and eloquence, and fine traits of character, and every endowment conferred upon them. There is need for them all in the arduous conflict. Then may we expect that " the wilderness and the solitary place shall be glad for them, and the desert shall rejoice and blossom as the rose." In this way may be realized the delightful anticipation, " Behold, I create a new heaven and a new earth ; and the former shall not be remembered, nor come into mind. Be ye glad and rejoice for ever in that which I create ; for, behold, I create Jerusalem a rejoicing, and her people a joy."

THE END.

www.ingramcontent.com/pod-product-compliance
Lightning Source LLC
Chambersburg PA
CBHW031157050726
47495CB00019B/2387